The Pughs' tavern

Rachel's parlor

RACHEL'S WORLD
Charles Town in 1724

Waterfront

MYSTERIES THROUGH TIME

MYSTERY ON SKULL ISLAND

by

Elizabeth McDavid Jones

an imprint of

WINDMILL
BOOKS
New York

Published in 2009 by Windmill Books, LLC
303 Park Avenue South, Suite # 1280, New York, NY 10010-3657

Cover and Map Illustrations: Dahl Taylor
Line Art: Greg Dearth

Photo Credit: Page 175, Hulton Archive/Getty Images

Publisher Cataloging Information

Jones, Elizabeth McDavid, 1958-
        Mystery on Skull Island / by Elizabeth McDavid Jones.
                p. cm. – (Mysteries through time)
        Summary: In 1724, twelve-year-old Rachel and her friend Sally discover a pirates' hiding place on a deserted island near Charles Town, South Carolina, and they suspect it may be connected to the woman who will soon become Rachel's stepmother.
                ISBN 978-1-60754-286-5 – ISBN 978-1-60754-302-2 (pbk.)
ISBN 978-1-60754-303-9 (6-pack)
                1. Charleston (S.C.)—History—Colonial period, ca. 1600-1775—Juvenile fiction
[1. Charleston (S.C.)—History—Colonial period, ca. 1600-1775—Fiction   2. Pirates—Fiction
3. Fathers and daughters—Fiction   4. Friendship—Fiction   5. Remarriage—Fiction] I. Title
II. Series
                [Fic]—dc22

Manufactured in the United States of America

To Peg Ross, my editor and teacher

TABLE OF CONTENTS

Chapter I
Pirates!

March 16, 1724

Twelve-year-old Rachel Howell leaned over the lee rail of the *Betsy Jo* and watched the white foam churning away from the ship's path like flowing cream. She gazed out over the great expanse of ocean that stretched before her as far as she could see. Somewhere out there was the coast of North Carolina, wild and mostly uninhabited—unless you counted Indians and pirates. And farther south—Rachel turned to look toward the starboard bow—was South Carolina and Charles Town, their destination.

"You shall love Charles Town," Rachel's father had promised in his letters. "You shall soon feel more at home here than you ever did in the city of New York." Rachel wasn't so sure about that. She'd overheard her grandparents call Charles Town "barely civilized." Rachel had lived with them in New York for the past seven years, ever since her mother died and her father went to Carolina to start a new life. Although her grandparents were remote and physically frail, their stately residence was the only home Rachel could remember.

A month ago, however, Rachel's father had sent for her to join him, hinting of some "wonderful news" he would tell her when she arrived. So here Rachel was, aboard the *Betsy Jo,* accompanied only by her grandfather's trusted slave Roland, bound for a strange place and a home with a father she barely knew. She *wanted* to go, of course—she had always dreamed of living with her father—but she couldn't help feeling scared and apprehensive. She had no idea what to expect in Charles Town.

Rachel listened to the slap and swish of water against the sides of the ship. How quickly the sea raced past; how boldly the *Betsy Jo* ran up and down the swell of each new wave and plunged into the next. "If only *I* could be so confident," Rachel muttered, as she fingered the teardrop pearl pendant around her neck. The necklace had been her mother's. Rachel wore it all the time and often fiddled with it when she felt nervous or insecure.

"Ah, there you are, Miss Rachel." It was Roland. Rachel hadn't noticed him coming up behind her. "I've looked all about the ship for you. To whom are you talking?"

Rachel turned to face the old black man who was more a friend than a servant. "Oh, no one, Roland. I was just wondering what Charles Town would be like."

"Different from anything we've ever seen, I imagine. Might be a little like New York harbor, maybe, but mostly different, missy, mostly different." He paused, leaned on the railing, and looked out across the water. "'Tis hot there, missy. That's all I know."

Rachel sighed. "I hope 'tis not *too* different. Nor too hot." She was watching the flickering crescents of sunlight on the waves. Then she thought she saw something white on the horizon, something more than just a crescent. "Look," she said to Roland, pointing into the distance. "What is that?"

Roland turned in the direction she pointed, but he didn't have a chance to answer her question.

"Sail on the starboard bow!" the lookout sang from the crow's nest high in the ship's rigging. And a moment later: "She's tall, Cap'n, and armed heavy!"

Rachel looked up at the poop deck where the captain was gazing through his spyglass at the ship that was now visible and coming toward them. The first mate was pacing back and forth on the poop deck, talking to the captain.

"She's changed course," Rachel heard the captain say. "I think she's after us. We'll try to run for it." The captain gave the order for every sail to be unfurled. Suddenly the ship's crew were everywhere, racing to obey, their feet thudding on deck, arms and legs scrambling into the rigging to hoist the sails.

Rachel glanced at Roland with alarm. "What's afoot? Why is the ship chasing us?"

Roland's expression was grave. He nodded out toward the tall ship steadily gaining on the *Betsy Jo*. "'Tis a pirate ship, Miss Rachel. And it means to take us as a prize."

Rachel's mouth went dry. "What will happen if it should overtake us?"

"I can't venture to say. Pirates are a bad lot, though some are worse than others. We may be lucky."

"You mean we may get away?"

Roland, staring at the fast-approaching ship, shook his head slowly. "I don't think so, Miss Rachel. But we may get away with our lives."

Rachel didn't know for how long a time the *Betsy Jo* fled and the pirates pursued. It seemed hours, though it must have been much less, for the sun scarcely moved. The captain shouted and cursed, the crew scurried about like so many mice, and Rachel stood with Roland, clutching the rail, and stared, her heart beating like the wings of a bird, as the pirate ship came closer and closer. At last it drew near enough for Rachel to see it clearly. The ship was taller than the *Betsy Jo,* two-masted and painted black with a white band all around. On its bulwark Rachel saw swivel guns and cannons, and from a spar its pirate flag, the Jolly Roger, snapped in the wind. Finally the ship came so close that Rachel could see the pirates on board, and one, who had to be the captain, with his chin up and his eyes blazing, called out: "Heave to!"

With a grinding and crashing the two vessels locked. Rachel's stomach turned as the pirates boarded the *Betsy Jo*. They wore loose-fitting duck trousers and long knives strapped to their hips. Some had earrings; some were barefoot. All were sunburned and rough-looking. Rachel shrank back against Roland as the pirates pushed the two of them along with the other passengers into the captain's cabin. One pirate guarded the door, while the others proceeded to transfer the *Betsy Jo*'s cargo into their own vessel.

A few of the passengers whispered among themselves, but Rachel was much too frightened to think of talking. Outside she heard the bumps and thuds of barrels and boxes coming up from the ship's hold, and the bark of voices and the heavy tramp of feet. Silently she prayed that the *Betsy Jo*'s cargo would be rich enough to satisfy the pirates, that they would leave the ship without bothering the passengers. Through the cabin's small windows she could see the sun beginning to set, turning the ocean red. The water's reflection hit the ceiling like dancing flames and gave the room an eerie glow. An omen, Rachel told herself, and she tried hard to make herself believe it was for good and not for bad.

At last the noises outside quieted. "Are they gone?" Rachel whispered to Roland. Roland shook his head, put a finger to his lips, and pointed to the window directly across from them. Rachel glanced that way and gasped. The pirate captain was looking right back at her through the window, his gaze as cold as the depths of the sea. Rachel stifled the scream that sprang to her throat and jerked her eyes away as if they'd been burned. "Oh, Roland," she said, "why does he stare so?"

"Figuring what to do with us, I would guess. To rob us, or—"

"Pray, don't say it," Rachel cut him off, terrified at the picture of violence that had jumped to her mind. She grasped Roland's hand tightly. "They *must* leave us alone. I must reach Charles Town. I must see Papa."

Roland nodded, but his lips were drawn tight.

Then Rachel heard voices growling outside the door. The latch rattled and the door swung open. Two pirates stood in the doorway. One of them was the pirate captain. Rachel watched his cold eyes sweep across the room of frightened passengers. "Lord help us!" one of the women wailed, and the child in her arms began to cry. Rachel herself was so scared she could hardly breathe.

"What is it you want of us?" a man spoke up.

For a long time the pirate captain, his face impassive, stared at the man. Rachel's eyes, against her will, dropped to the cutlass at the pirate's side; then she quickly looked away, as if her gaze might remind the pirate of his sword. After endless minutes the pirate spoke. "Ah, what do I want of ye?" His voice was deep and laced with brogue. "Your jewelry, shoe buckles, coins, weapons. Anything of value." He paced across the room, scanning the knot of passengers. "Give your trinkets to my mate, and I won't let him harm ye."

Then, to Rachel's horror, the pirate captain stopped right in front of her. Roland pulled Rachel toward himself. "She's but a girl. Let her be," Roland said.

"I won't touch her if she hands over that necklace," the pirate said.

Unconsciously Rachel's fingers flew to her pendant. Her father had given it to her mother on their wedding day, and it was all Rachel had of her mother's. How could she turn it over to pirates? Rachel felt Roland's hands on her shoulders. "Give him the necklace, Miss Rachel." Roland's voice was gentle but firm.

Rachel felt sick, but with her hands trembling, she reached back to unfasten the necklace. Her fingers brushed across the broken pearl near the clasp as she undid it, and a lump rose in her throat. She felt as if she were giving away a part of herself. She dropped the necklace into the pirate's outstretched hand. He nodded, closed his fingers around Rachel's precious pendant, then tossed it indifferently to his mate, who had finished collecting valuables from the other passengers. One woman was crying over the loss of her brooch. Part of Rachel felt like crying, too, but another part felt only loathing for the pirates and their robbery. Then, without another word, the pirates backed out the door and were gone. There was more shouting outside, heavy footsteps, then stillness.

"I think they *are* gone now," Roland murmured to Rachel. "Are you well enough?"

Rachel was shaking, and a nod was all she could manage. She felt wretched over her pendant, but she knew that wasn't what Roland meant.

As if reading her thoughts, Roland patted Rachel's arm and said, "Better your necklace than your life, missy."

"Yes," said the woman who had been crying over her brooch. She sniffed and wiped her tears with her handkerchief. "At least we're all alive."

"Let us hope our captain and crew are in the same state," said a man. He and some of the other male passengers ventured out to investigate. They found the captain and crew locked in the ship's hold but unharmed.

Since the pirates had done no damage to the *Betsy Jo,* the ship lay at anchor for the night and resumed its journey in the morning. On the following day, Rachel watched the shore of South Carolina come into view, green and welcome as paradise. Rachel wanted nothing more than to feel her feet steady on solid ground and to look into her father's face.

It was early afternoon when the *Betsy Jo* finally reached Charles Town. The town was situated on a peninsula between two rivers, the Cooper and the Ashley. The harbor was on the Cooper River and deep enough for the *Betsy Jo* to sail right up to the dock. Rachel's first view of her new home was of ships' masts poking up everywhere, swaying back and forth as the ships moved with the current. The wharf was lined with warehouses and jammed with people, both black and white—sailors and laborers, slaves, passengers and merchants, people coming and going, standing, hurrying, loading and unloading. And all around and in and out, various vehicles made their way through the crowd: drays and barrows, lumbering sledges and handcarts.

When Rachel stepped with Roland off the *Betsy Jo*'s gangway onto the quay, she felt she'd be smothered, either by the throngs of people or by the close-pressing heat, unstirred by ocean breezes she'd felt onboard the ship. When she'd left New York, there was snow on the ground. Here the damp, unmoving air weighed upon her like a mound of woolen blankets. And it was only March. What would it be like, she wondered, when summer arrived?

A host of smells seemed to jump out at her: hot tar, sour mud, rotting fish, and, most of all, sweat. Everywhere there was sweat, glistening on the faces of people hurrying by, dripping from the backs of slaves loading barrels of rice onto a ship. Already tiny beads of perspiration showed on Roland's forehead.

"One thing you were right about," she said to Roland. "'Tis indeed hot." Rachel squinted against the bright sunlight and let her eyes run over the crowd. "How shall we ever find my father amidst all these people?"

"I imagine your papa will find you," Roland said, "if we stay here near the *Betsy Jo.*"

At that very moment, a tall man in a bright blue broadcloth coat squeezed his way between a knot of chatting women and some bundles of staves stacked on the wharf. The man looked right at Rachel and Roland, then up at the *Betsy Jo,* and a puzzled expression came over his face. Rachel felt a rush of breathlessness. Was this Papa? It had been so long since she'd seen him.

The man approached them hesitantly. Rachel's heart gave a little jump. "Papa?" she said, feeling suddenly shy.

"Rachel?" A spark came to the man's eyes. "Rachel!" He strode forward and clasped his arms around her. "Oh, 'tis fine to see you!"

With her father's embrace, Rachel's shyness departed, and her words tumbled out. "Oh, Papa, 'tis wonderful to see you, too. But, Papa, I lost Mama's necklace. It has near broke my heart."

Mr. Howell's face fell. "Oh, surely not. That necklace meant so much to your mother."

"I beg your pardon, sir," said Roland, "but she didn't really lose it. It was stole by pirates."

"You were attacked by pirates?" Mr. Howell's brows drew up in concern. "And you escaped unharmed. Everyone did, I imagine?" He looked at Roland.

"Yes, sir. They robbed us clean, but all are fine."

"Well, thank God for that. Pirates and Charles Town have had a long history together. Blackbeard, Stede Bonnet, Richard Worley—they've all tried a hand at terrorizing us. Once Blackbeard blockaded the entire harbor and held our most prominent citizens for ransom. But that was more than five years ago, and since then our government has cracked down hard on piracy. The council tried and hanged forty-nine pirates in one month alone."

"Are there so very many pirates in these waters, Papa?" asked Rachel.

"Not only on the waters, daughter, but in the town itself. Pirates are suffered by the merchants and townsfolk alike for the money they spend. The rascals are not nearly as bold as they once were. Still, they're a threat to shipping, as you saw." Then his voice changed to a much warmer tone. "Enough of pirates. 'Tis sad you've lost the pendant, but you're here at long last, and safe." Mr. Howell put his arm around Rachel and squeezed. "'Twill be wonderful having you with me, my dear."

Rachel was too happy to speak. She couldn't believe she had ever worried about this moment. It felt so natural to be with her father. It was as if they had never been separated. Then Mr. Howell said something that brought Rachel up short.

"We shall be a family, all of us."

Rachel stared at her father, not sure she had heard correctly. "All of us?"

Mr. Howell, with a glint in his eye, smiled. "That's the news of which I wrote you. I'm engaged to be married. You're to have a new mother."

CHAPTER 2
STEPMOTHER

Rachel felt as if the breath had been knocked out of her. She'd thought she was to have Papa back, all to herself, after so many years apart. Tears welled in Rachel's eyes, but she blinked them back. "When, Papa?" she managed to choke out, then, almost as an afterthought, she added, "To whom?"

"In late June, to a young lady from Philadelphia named Miranda LeBoyer. But she's coming to Charles Town much sooner, in a matter of weeks."

"Oh." Rachel didn't know what else to say.

"Miranda and her aunt will be staying with us until the wedding. 'Twill be a chance for you and Miranda to become acquainted." Mr. Howell looked very pleased with these arrangements, and Rachel did her best to hide her burning disappointment.

"Just think, my dear," Mr. Howell went on happily, "what it will be like to have a mother again. I wanted to provide that for you before I brought you here." He patted Rachel's hand. "You shall soon grow to care for her as much as I do."

Rachel tried to smile. Papa expected her to be pleased, and the least Rachel could do was pretend that she was.

Later, as their carriage rattled through Charles Town's streets and Mr. Howell pointed out landmarks, Rachel couldn't help but let her spirits rise. Charles Town was indeed a beautiful city, drastically different from anything she had seen before. "'Tis the West Indies trade and its influence," Mr. Howell explained, "which makes us unique among the colonies."

Indeed, the houses they passed reminded Rachel of a spring garden, their exteriors painted in shades of pink, green, yellow, and blue and adorned with balconies, tile roofs, and multilevel verandas. There were the narrow "single houses," one room wide so the wind could blow all the way through, and the newer, more elaborate "double houses," with a long interior hall down the middle called a breezeway. Rachel shivered as her father called her attention to a particular double house on Church Street. "'Twas once a pirate haunt," he said, "in the days when we welcomed the scoundrels for the Spanish gold they brought to town. Not so long ago, really."

The Howell residence was farther up the same street, built of brick, three stories tall and situated against the street. "There's a large courtyard in back," Mr. Howell

said, nodding toward a decorated brick wall adjoining
the house. Through the gate, Rachel could see huge oaks
and the strange, fanlike foliage of the trees her father
called palmettos. "It looks lovely," Rachel said. "Might
I walk there sometimes?"

"Whenever the fancy strikes you," Mr. Howell said
with a smile. Then he added, "I fear you'll be much on
your own, Rachel. My shipping business keeps me occupied during the day, but there will be servants to see to
your needs, and Mistress Brownlow, the housekeeper,
lodges with us. Though she's very busy—and she'll be
the first to tell you so—I've instructed her to assist you
and answer any questions you may have. I want you to
feel that you may do as you please, within reason. After all,
my dear, this is your home."

Home. Coming from Papa's lips, the word sounded
wonderful to Rachel. She silently vowed not to allow
worrisome thoughts of future stepmothers to intrude
upon her present happiness. After all, she told herself,
it would be months before the wedding took place and
weeks before Miss LeBoyer even arrived. A great deal
could happen in so long a time. A *very* great deal.

The following day, Rachel walked with Papa the
few blocks to Saint Philip's Church to attend Sunday

services. Rachel had seen the church's spire from her bedroom window. Afterward, they dined with friends of Mr. Howell's and, in the evening, when the day's heat had relented, took a long walk to familiarize Rachel with the neighborhood. "You'll want to take your exercise in the morning, before it gets hot," Papa told her. "Springtime in Charles Town is much warmer than what you're accustomed to. You may walk in the courtyard, as I said, or go about the town a bit, as long as you don't go far. One of the servants will accompany you, if you like."

On Monday Roland was to board a ship to return to New York, and Rachel rose early that morning to go with Papa to see Roland off. The day was overcast and held a hint of rain, but the air was so delightfully cool that Rachel wanted to walk. Papa walked with her, while Roland, who suffered from rheumatism when the weather changed, was sent ahead in the carriage. They went down Church Street, past the same fine homes Rachel had seen before, then turned toward the bay on Tradd Street, where many of the residents kept shops in their homes. Rachel saw signs for millinery shops and dry-goods stores, candle makers and shoemakers, silversmiths and pewterers.

Toward the end of the street, they stopped at a confectioner's and bought apple tarts and pastries that Papa called Barbados sweetmeats. As they were leaving the shop, Papa stopped to talk to two gentlemen whom he introduced to Rachel as fellow shipping merchants. Rachel tried to listen politely but their talk was of turpentine prices and import duties, and Rachel quickly became bored. She went outside and stood on the oyster-shell sidewalk, watching the coming and going of passersby.

"Good morning to you." The voice at Rachel's back jerked her attention away from the scene on the street. She turned around to see who had spoken to her. A girl about Rachel's age but taller than Rachel was standing in the doorway next to the confectioner's. She was wearing a mob cap and a calico gown with a kerchief around her neck and an apron at her waist. She had a basket on one arm. "Are you Mr. Howell's daughter?"

"Why, yes," said Rachel, a little startled that the girl knew who she was.

The girl nodded emphatically. "I thought as much. We heard you was coming." She smiled broadly. "I was sweeping out the doorway a minute ago and saw you both go into Mistress Bolton's."

Rachel assumed Mistress Bolton was the owner of the confection shop. "How do you know my father?" Rachel asked.

"He's one of my mother's customers. Most everyone who works nearby is. Our tavern has a goodly reputation throughout Charles Town, but especially here, near the bay. I do the cooking myself . . . well, some of it, to be sure. My sister, Prudence, does a fair portion as well. How long have you been in town?"

"I only just arrived," Rachel answered. "On Saturday."

"How was your voyage?"

Before Rachel could answer, a redheaded boy who looked to be seven or eight popped out of the tavern doorway behind the girl. "Sally," he said, "you've not left yet. I want to go to the market with you. Mama said that I might."

Sally heaved a great sigh, which made Rachel think the boy, who must be Sally's brother, was a great vexation. "Must you come with me *everywhere,* Todd? I can scarce answer nature without you underfoot."

"I'll not trouble you, I promise," said the boy earnestly.

"'Tis what you say every time, and every time you trouble me. I'll take you only if you promise to stay by my side. No running off to gawk at ships or talk to sailors. Y'understand?"

Todd agreed.

Sally turned back to Rachel. "Would you care to come with us, Miss Howell? 'Twould be nice to keep company with someone my own age for a change. Small boys tend to be rather poor at conversation."

Rachel felt a rush of eagerness to go along. She hadn't realized how lonely she'd felt with no one to whom she could really talk. She was sorry to have to turn down Sally's offer. Rachel explained why she couldn't join them, then said, "I would love to come upon another occasion, if I might."

"Of course," Sally said, "visit whenever you like. Pray, come tomorrow. I'll show you about the town."

Rachel hesitated. She wasn't entirely sure how much freedom she was to have. In New York her grandparents had been very strict. Rachel had had a governess who rarely let her out of sight. Yet Papa had said that here she might come and go as she pleased, and Rachel very much wanted a friend. "I should like that," Rachel finally said. "I shall try to come."

About that time, Papa emerged from the confectioner's. "My apologies, Rachel," he said. "I never expected to be so long. We must make haste to the docks lest Roland's ship leave before we arrive." Then he seemed to notice Sally and Todd. "How does your mother, children? I trust she's well?"

"Aye, sir," Sally answered. "She's right well."

"Good day to you, then," he said. "Come along, Rachel."

"Good day," Rachel said to Sally, and smiled. She hoped Sally knew the smile meant she would be back tomorrow if there were any way she possibly could.

Rachel was happy to find the next day that, true to Papa's word, she was free to do much as she wanted. After breakfast, Papa left to inspect his warehouses, and Mistress Brownlow promptly informed Rachel that the entire household would be busy taking up the rugs and storing them for the summer, and it would do well for Rachel to stay out of their way. Rachel proclaimed she was going for a walk and then fled gleefully into the crisp morning air. She hurried the few blocks to Tradd Street and found the tavern without any trouble.

Rachel hesitated at the door, uncertain whether to knock or just enter. She decided to knock, but as no one answered she pushed open the door and went in. She found herself standing inside a large room with a number of wooden tables and chairs throughout, a serving bar on one side, and a fireplace in the middle of the far wall. Against one wall was a walnut desk where a woman sat writing with a quill pen in a ledger book. The woman was dressed in a plain brown bodice and an apron fastened with pins. She looked up as Rachel came in. "Then I did hear someone knock," she said. "I thought my ears was playing tricks on me. Never heard of knocking at a tavern door."

"I—I wasn't sure of the custom for entering," Rachel stammered. "I've never been in a tavern before. I am looking for Sally, if you please."

Then the woman stood up and approached Rachel. "You must be Mr. Howell's daughter. Sally told me you might pay us a visit. I'm Mistress Pugh, Sally's mother." Smiling, she extended her hand to Rachel.

"How do you do, ma'am," said Rachel, curtsying and

taking Mistress Pugh's hand. "My name is Rachel."

"I'm right glad to meet you, Rachel. I hope you'll come here often. Sally is out in the kitchen house, cleaning up from breakfast. Go back through the door there." She indicated a door in the back of the room.

Rachel went through the door out to a porch and down the steps into a covered brick walkway through the garden. At the end of the walkway was the kitchen house. The door stood open to the morning breeze. Inside, Rachel saw Sally at the pine table washing dishes in an enamel tub. Sally greeted Rachel heartily. "I'm so glad you came. Mama said I might have the whole morning free to show you around, and she asked Prudence to watch Todd so he won't pester us."

"Why, I think Todd's delightful," Rachel said.

"He's delightful for perhaps a quarter of an hour," said Sally, "which is about how long he'll mind you before he runs off on his own and starts getting into mischief. With him along, we'd have not a minute to ourselves to get acquainted. This way we can talk."

And talk they did. Rachel found it easier to talk to Sally than to anyone she had ever known. Sally showed her all over Charles Town, from the warehouses and the slave market on the wharves to the fashionable shops and homes on east Broad Street. At the head of Broad, Sally pointed out the guardhouse. "That's where they kept Stede Bonnet imprisoned till they hanged him for piracy,"

Sally casually told Rachel. Rachel shivered. Would she never hear the end of pirates in Charles Town?

At noon the girls sat on the seawall overlooking the bay and ate the ham and biscuits Mistress Pugh had packed for them, while seagulls wheeled and cried above their heads. Rachel felt as if she had known Sally for years rather than only a few hours. They talked endlessly, about everything imaginable. Rachel even found herself telling Sally her fears about having a stepmother. Sally sympathized but advised Rachel to make the best of it. "Perhaps your stepmother will turn out to be better than you think," Sally suggested.

"Perhaps," said Rachel. She only wished she could make herself believe it.

Over the next few weeks, Rachel went to visit Sally nearly every day. She helped Sally with her chores in the tavern, even trying her hand at the cooking, which Rachel found she enjoyed. She went with Sally on errands for her mother, sometimes to shop for meat or fowl at the market on the corner of Church and Broad, sometimes to take the tavern linens to the laundress. Rachel enjoyed talking to Mistress Pugh almost as much as she did to Sally. She grew fond of Todd and really didn't mind his tagging along.

At mealtimes at home, Rachel chattered to Papa about her new friendships. He seemed glad that she had made friends, though one night he remarked that he soon must see to Rachel's schooling. Rachel was jarred; she had grown accustomed to her liberty, and for a while she worried over the prospect of having to give it up for the confinement of school. As the days went by, though, and Papa didn't mention it again, Rachel began to hope that he had forgotten about it.

Papa seemed to make an effort to spend time with Rachel every evening, if only for an hour or so. Sometimes he read aloud to her. Other times they played a game of backgammon or checkers.

One evening as they were finishing supper, Papa pushed his chair back from the table and told Rachel he had something important to tell her. Rachel noticed the gleam in his eye and had the sinking feeling that her days of freedom had come to an end. Papa had enrolled her in school; she was sure of it. "Yes, Papa?" she said, bracing herself to hear the bad news.

To her surprise, Papa laughed. "My dear, don't look so glum. 'Tis good news, I assure you."

"Good news?" Rachel had learned by now that she and Papa had different ideas of what constituted good news.

"Indeed," Papa said. "I have word the *Dominion* is waiting outside the harbor for the pilots to lead her in first thing in the morning."

Rachel relaxed. She'd been worried for nothing. The *Dominion* must be one of her father's ships. "Is she bringing a rich cargo, Papa?"

Papa smiled broadly. "In a manner of speaking, yes. Miss LeBoyer is aboard. Get a good night's rest, daughter. You'll meet your new mother tomorrow."

CHAPTER 3

SCOUNDREL IN THE PARLOR

 Rachel did anything but get a good night's rest. She thought she would much rather face school tomorrow than her future stepmother. She tossed and turned for hours. She didn't remember falling asleep at all; she simply jerked awake with light streaming through her window, plagued with a feeling of disquiet and the vague impression that she'd been dreaming of pirates.

When Rachel went downstairs for breakfast, though, Papa told her a west wind had blown all night and was blowing still, preventing the *Dominion* from sailing into the harbor. Papa seemed disappointed, but Rachel wasn't sure how she felt. A part of her was relieved at the delay, but another part of her just wanted to be done with the meeting.

They were finishing the midday meal when Papa got word that the wind had changed and the *Dominion* was on its way in. Rachel felt new, sharp pangs of anxiety, and she reached for her pendant, only to find, of course, that it was not there. As the carriage carrying Papa and Rachel to the wharf bumped through the streets of Charles Town, Rachel did her best to convince herself that she was worrying for nothing, that she would like Miss LeBoyer as much as Papa said she would.

After all, hadn't Rachel been just as worried about her own reunion with Papa and her arrival in Charles Town? And look at the way that had turned out. Rachel was happier with Papa than she had ever been with her stiff, formal grandparents, and Charles Town was as familiar to Rachel now as if she had lived here all her life.

'Twill be the same way with Miss LeBoyer, Rachel told herself firmly. *In a month's time I shall feel as comfortable around her as I do in Charles Town.*

This thought bolstered Rachel's courage considerably, at least until the carriage rattled to a stop at the wharf. The harbor, as usual, was crowded with ships riding at anchor. Papa pointed out a sleek schooner he said was the *Dominion.* As the *Dominion*'s passengers began to disembark, Rachel watched Papa's eyes dart eagerly from face to face. Finally she saw his face light up with recognition. Rachel followed his gaze to a pretty young woman in a yellow silk gown coming down the gangway, who must be Miss LeBoyer. She walked arm in arm with an elderly woman wearing a gauze cap with frilled edges—obviously

Aunt Catherine. Rachel stared at Miss LeBoyer. How young she looked! She couldn't be too much older than Sally's sister, Prudence, who was seventeen.

"There, 'tis she," Papa said. There was something in his voice that made a flicker of jealousy dart through Rachel, though it quickly gave way to an overwhelming shyness. Suddenly Rachel had the urge to cling to Papa's arm as if she were five years old.

She couldn't, of course, for Papa was taking Miss LeBoyer's hand, greeting her and Aunt Catherine, introducing them to Rachel. Rachel knew she should greet Miss LeBoyer, but her tongue was thick in her mouth and wouldn't move.

"'Tis a pleasure to meet you, Rachel," Miss LeBoyer said, smiling down at Rachel and extending her hand.

Rachel made herself accept Miss LeBoyer's outstretched hand. "The pleasure is mine," Rachel said. She hoped it didn't sound as stiff as it felt.

"Mr. Howell, your daughter is a dear," Aunt Catherine said. Then she patted Rachel's cheek and repeated the same thing to Rachel by way of a greeting: "You are a dear."

Rachel, unsure how to respond, stammered, "Thank you, madame," and heartily wished that all this was over and she was in the courtyard at home in her favorite spot under the big magnolia tree.

At last the luggage had been loaded on top of the carriage and Rachel, Papa, Miss LeBoyer, and her aunt had

all climbed inside and were on their way back through
the streets of Charles Town. Rachel stared out the window
while the adults discussed the sea voyage and Charles
Town's weather. For once she was glad that children were
expected to remain quiet, for she felt very uncomfortable
sitting next to Miss LeBoyer and didn't think she would
know what to say to her if she were obliged to speak.

Then the adults fell silent, and Miss LeBoyer turned
to Rachel. "You're twelve, are you not, Rachel?" Then,
without waiting for an answer, she said, "When I was
your age, I enjoyed needlework. Have you anything you've
been working on lately?"

Rachel hated needlework. In New York, Grandmother
had insisted that she learn embroidery, but Rachel had
never been good at it, and she hadn't once picked up
the sampler she had brought with her to Charles Town.
She knew, though, that Miss LeBoyer was trying to be
nice, so she responded by saying, "No, Miss LeBoyer,
nothing lately."

"You must call me Miranda." Miss LeBoyer was
attempting to set her at ease, Rachel knew, but she didn't
like the thought of being forced to be so familiar with
a complete stranger. It made her feel even more awkward
than before. She struggled for something to say.

Thankfully, at that moment Aunt Catherine, who was
looking out the carriage window, mentioned her surprise
at seeing Charles Town ladies so fashionably dressed.

"Yes," Papa said, smiling. "'Tis said our ladies rival Londoners for the gayness of their dress." Miss LeBoyer joined in the conversation, and Rachel gratefully turned her attention to the scene outside.

The carriage soon turned onto Tradd Street, and Rachel caught a glimpse of Sally and Todd walking along the sidewalk. She leaned out of the carriage window and waved. Sally waved back.

Immediately Rachel felt Miss LeBoyer's eyes upon her. "Who are *they*?" she asked.

Rachel winced at Miss LeBoyer's scornful tone. "They're my friends," she said stoutly. Rachel glanced back at Sally and Todd, diminishing in size as the carriage sped away. She noticed for the first time that they were barefoot.

"Oh, I see." Miss LeBoyer said nothing more, but her lips were drawn together tightly. Rachel was sure she disapproved of Sally and Todd, and she had a disturbing feeling that her future stepmother was not the kind of person who would long keep such opinions to herself.

As soon as the carriage pulled through the driveway gate to the side of the house, the footman met them with the news that Papa's new business partner, Mr. Craven, was waiting in the parlor to see him.

"Is he, then?" Papa looked surprised. The footman was

helping Miss LeBoyer and Aunt Catherine from the carriage. "It must be important," Papa said to Miss LeBoyer as she descended the carriage steps. "I've never known Craven to venture far from his home or the wharves. A bit of a recluse he is, but one of Charles Town's shrewdest businessmen. One of the wealthiest also. I must admit I was flattered when Craven approached me about joining him in his latest shipping venture to Barbados. It took most of my capital to do so, but I expect to make my investment back three or four times over again."

"It sounds as if I'm to marry a very shrewd businessman myself," Miss LeBoyer said with admiration in her voice.

"Let us hope at least a competent one," Papa replied, beaming. "Come. I'd like you to meet my partner while you have the chance."

He took Miss LeBoyer on one arm and Aunt Catherine on the other and started toward the house, leaving Rachel standing on the carriage step. A moment passed before she noticed the footman with his arm outstretched to help her down; until now, it had always been Papa who took her arm at the carriage door and walked her into the house. Rachel bit her lip and told herself Papa was only being polite to their guests. She accepted the footman's arm and followed the adults inside.

᭦

Mr. Craven was seated on the velvet settee in the parlor. He rose when they walked in, and Rachel was instantly struck by the massive size of his wig. It was the largest Rachel had ever seen—waves of white on top of great long curls that cascaded onto his shoulders and flowed down his back. Though Craven was portly, the wig made him appear much larger than he really was, and Rachel thought it didn't fit his sharp, narrow face. She was sure Craven wore the wig only to impress people with his wealth. She had never cared for such putting on of airs, and she didn't think she cared much for Mr. Craven, even if he was her father's business partner. The man had a strange gaze, as if his small, pale eyes could see right through a person. Rachel wanted to get out of his presence, but she knew she couldn't politely leave the room until the introductions had been made.

As Rachel expected, Papa introduced the ladies first. Mr. Craven's manner was buttery smooth as he greeted Aunt Catherine, but it was polished silver once he turned to Papa's fiancée. "Ah, Miss LeBoyer," he said, "your loveliness rivals that of Charles Town itself." He bowed and kissed the young woman's hand.

Rachel blinked. Had she seen Miss LeBoyer cringe at Mr. Craven's touch, or had she only imagined it? Maybe Miss LeBoyer felt the same way about Mr. Craven as Rachel did. Rachel warmed to her future stepmother just a bit. Perhaps she *could* call her Miranda.

Then Papa introduced Rachel. Turning her eyes from Mr. Craven's odd gaze, Rachel mumbled, "How do you do," then excused herself. "I have a sampler to work," she said, with a quick glance at Miranda. Rachel intended the words as a good-faith offering, but Miranda was caught up in conversation and didn't seem to hear.

Rachel hurried upstairs to her room to search for the sampler. She found it in her trunk, buried underneath her winter woolens. She took up needle and thread and settled in a chair to work, but somehow her attention kept drifting to the open window, where a soft sea breeze ruffled the curtains. Outside, a mockingbird sang from a tree bursting with yellow blooms. It was the same problem Rachel always had with her samplers: she simply couldn't sit inside and sew when other, more interesting activities beckoned— which was most of the time.

Yet Rachel was determined to make this effort to please Miranda. Perhaps it would be easier to concentrate outside in Rachel's favorite spot under the magnolia tree. She gathered her sewing and went downstairs. In the hallway, she passed Mistress Brownlow complaining to Papa about "that saucy Becky," one of the servant girls.

"Mistress Brownlow, really, you must handle this yourself," Papa was saying. Rachel heard the strained impatience in his voice—it was hard to believe Mistress Brownlow would disturb Papa for such a trifle—and she hurried past them through the back door into the courtyard.

Rachel had just sat down under the tree when she noticed that the parlor window above her head was open and she could hear the murmur of conversation inside. Her first instinct was to get up and go elsewhere, for she had no intention of eavesdropping. But the lowered voices caught her attention. The voices belonged to Mr. Craven and Miranda—apparently Aunt Catherine had gone upstairs—and they seemed to be trying to keep their conversation private.

"I wondered if you recognized me," Mr. Craven was saying.

"Does a scoundrel change so much in a matter of years?"

Had Rachel heard right? Had Miranda called Craven a scoundrel? Miranda's voice was so low, Rachel thought perhaps she'd misheard.

Then Rachel heard Craven laugh. "Oh, but I *have* changed, my dear. I'm a businessman now."

"Pray tell me, something honest this time?"

But Rachel never heard Craven's answer. Apparently Papa had satisfied Mistress Brownlow and come back to the parlor. "Pardon the interruption," he said. "I hope you had a chance to get acquainted."

"Oh . . . quite," Miranda stammered. "I . . . uh . . . was inquiring about hurricanes in Charles Town. I understand there was quite a nasty one a few years back."

Rachel leaped to her feet in disgust, sending the sampler tumbling from her lap. Miranda was lying to Papa!

"Yes, as I was saying," said Mr. Craven, "our genteel life here does have its drawbacks, though they are few."

That's not at all what he was saying! Rachel's lips moved with the words, though she didn't pronounce them aloud. Why were Mr. Craven and Miranda pretending to Papa that they didn't know each other?

Now Rachel no longer cared if she was eavesdropping. As quietly as she could, she moved to stand right under the window, her back pressed against the wall of the house. She wanted to hear every word that was said in that parlor.

The conversation went on, and the talk turned to Miranda's journey, Papa's investment in Craven's business, and the upcoming wedding. Perhaps now the two of them would mention their acquaintance, Rachel thought. But they didn't.

And then Mr. Craven was taking his leave, and Papa and Miranda were alone in the parlor. "What do you think of my business partner?" Papa asked.

Rachel held her breath. Would Miranda tell Papa the truth, now that they were alone?

"He seems very distinguished," Miranda answered. Then she yawned. "Oh dear, I hadn't realized how exhausted I am. Would you think it terribly uncivil of me if I went upstairs and napped before supper?"

"Not at all," Papa said. "I have some business papers I need to go over in my office. I shall look forward to seeing you refreshed and beautiful as usual at supper."

In a swish of skirts Miranda was gone. Rachel's pulse beat in her throat. Clearly Miranda was *not* going to tell Papa about her acquaintance with Mr. Craven. Even worse, Rachel suddenly realized, Miranda was *not* going to tell Papa that she knew something unfavorable about Mr. Craven's dealings in the past.

As his business partner, Papa needed to know if Craven had been dishonest, Rachel reasoned. "*Somebody* should tell him," she whispered. "And if Miranda won't, then I shall."

CHAPTER 4
BANNED!

Rachel whirled and hurried inside the house. But she was too late. Papa had already disappeared into his office across the hall from the parlor.

Rachel stood outside the office door a long time, debating with herself about what she should do. Papa had made it clear from the first that she was never to disturb him in this room. Rachel had not yet seen Papa angry, and she didn't care to do so. Perhaps she should wait until he came out, she thought. But then it would be suppertime, and after supper he would probably be entertaining Miranda and Aunt Catherine. Rachel might not get another chance to talk to him alone. She took a deep breath and knocked on the door.

"I'm busy, Mistress Brownlow," Papa called from within. "Handle it yourself, I told you." Papa sounded extremely vexed, and for a moment Rachel considered fleeing. But Miranda's voice echoed in her mind—*Something honest this time?*—and Rachel took a deep breath and spoke. "'Tis I, Papa, not Mistress Brownlow. May I come in?"

"Rachel, yes, yes. Come in," he said.

He doesn't *sound* angry, Rachel told herself. That gave her courage, and she turned the knob and pushed the door open. She had never been inside Papa's office before. The room was wainscoted in heavy cypress paneling; deep-red draperies hung from the window. On one wall, glass-fronted bookcases stuffed with thick volumes rose from floor to ceiling. All the furniture was of dark mahogany, including Papa's massive desk in the corner and the revolving drum table next to it, set with a globe. The room had a heavy, masculine air. Rachel felt intimidated, even by Papa, so unfamiliar in his spectacles and the turban he wore when relaxing in private. He looked every bit a barrister or a judge, not at all like her papa. "Now, daughter," he said, looking at her over the top of his spectacles, "tell me what is so important that it can't wait until suppertime."

Papa's manner struck Rachel as unusually stern, and her courage started to ebb. The speech she had planned so carefully flew right out of her head. All her concerns about Craven suddenly seemed flimsy. What could she say, really? That she didn't like Craven because he looked at her oddly and his wig was too big? That she thought he *might* be dishonest because she *might* have heard Miranda call him a scoundrel? It all sounded ridiculous, even to Rachel. She'd been far too eager to jump to conclusions, she decided.

All she really knew for sure was that Craven and Miranda knew each other and were pretending that they didn't. This is what she told Papa.

"Is that what's troubling you?" he said. "'Tis entirely possible that they *have* met. Mr. Craven is from Barbados, and Miranda was born there, though her family emigrated to Philadelphia some years ago."

"Then why wouldn't they admit that they were acquainted?"

"I doubt 'tis a matter of admitting or not admitting their acquaintance, Rachel. Miranda was but a girl then. They couldn't have known each other well."

Papa's answer didn't really satisfy Rachel, though she didn't know how to say so without sounding impertinent. But she couldn't ignore her lingering discomfort about Craven. "Are . . . are you certain you can trust Mr. Craven, Papa?"

Papa stiffened. "Why shouldn't I trust him?"

"I don't know," she stammered. "He . . . looked at me so strangely. It made me feel uneasy, I suppose."

"Oh, that." Papa smiled slightly. "Yes, it does give one an odd feeling the first time he looks at you." He paused. "Craven has but one good eye, you see. He lost his vision in the other eye in a duel long ago. As for his

integrity, the man is beyond reproach. He's a member
of the Assembly, and one of Charles Town's most prominent citizens. I am honored to do business with him,
I assure you.

"Now, I really must get back to work, Rachel. Unless
there is something else?"

Papa's voice had an irritated edge, and Rachel was
afraid she had pushed him too far. "No, sir. There is
nothing else." She backed out of the library and closed
the door.

Rachel was miserable at supper that evening. In the
first place, her usual spot at the table, to Papa's right,
was now occupied by Aunt Catherine. Miranda sat to
Papa's left and Rachel was assigned to the other side
of Aunt Catherine, farther from Papa than anyone else.
The seating was arranged according to status and was
proper, Rachel knew, but she couldn't help feeling as if
she had been banished from Papa's presence. It didn't
help that now, with Aunt Catherine and Miranda present,
Papa would expect Rachel to remain silent unless she
was addressed by one of the adults. And no one seemed
to be addressing her.

Rachel looked toward the long dining room windows.
The evening was growing dark. Shadows thrown by the

candles in their stands fluttered on the papered walls. In came two servant girls bearing dessert: sugar figs and a syllabub. One of the girls was the "saucy Becky" of whom Mistress Brownlow had been complaining. Rachel liked Becky quite a lot; she hoped Papa had not let Mistress Brownlow punish her.

Rachel's attention snapped back to the table when she heard Papa say her name. "Rachel? Are you going to answer Aunt Catherine?"

"I beg your pardon," Rachel said quickly. "What was it you asked, Aunt?"

"I was wondering how you spend your days, dear."

"How I spend my days?" Rachel was at a loss. She *couldn't* tell Aunt Catherine that she spent most of her time at the tavern and going about town with Sally and Todd. "Well, I walk a great deal," Rachel said. She paused. She knew she had to say more than that. No one could spend the entire day walking. She wracked her brain for some other wholesome activity that would account for her long absences from the house. "And sometimes I visit friends—" she started, then stopped abruptly when she saw Miranda frown. Too late Rachel realized her mistake. Now Miranda was sure to voice her disapproval of Rachel's barefoot friends. Rachel felt sick. It seemed as if all she'd done all day was say the wrong things. She dropped her eyes and stared at her plate, waiting for Miranda to speak.

But it was Aunt Catherine she heard. "You do no lessons, child? No reading?"

"I read some," said Rachel miserably. "But I have no lessons to do."

Aunt Catherine raised her eyebrows. She turned to Papa. "Are there no schools for girls in Charles Town?"

"Oh, yes, there are several fine establishments," Papa said. "I've been intending to see to Rachel's education, but I've been so busy . . ." He cleared his throat and said, "I'll make some inquiries into which school is best and enroll her straightaway."

"I think that would be wise, John." It was Miranda. She glanced quickly at Rachel before saying more. Rachel knew what was coming.

"'Tis important," Miranda went on, "that your daughter associate only with girls of her own station. Your reputation is at stake as much as Rachel's. I don't think it proper that she be seen with . . . street urchins."

Rachel's temper flared. She sat bolt upright in her chair. Sally and Todd were not street urchins! But she didn't dare speak.

"I wasn't aware that my daughter was keeping such company," Papa said. "Rachel?" He gave Rachel a questioning gaze.

"She means Sally and Todd, Papa." Rachel wanted to defend herself, defend her friends, but she didn't want to press Papa as she had done this afternoon. She could only hope that, since Papa knew Mistress Pugh, he wouldn't share Miranda's opinion of her friends.

"Mistress Pugh's children? Why, she keeps a tavern but I hardly think—"

"Mercy sakes, Mr. Howell," Aunt Catherine cut in. "'Twill never do for your daughter to associate with the offspring of a tavern keeper. You must think of Rachel's future, her prospects for a suitable marriage. She may be young, but she must begin now to move in the proper social circles."

"You're right, of course," said Papa somewhat sheepishly. "I suppose I'm not yet adept at being a proper father."

Indignation rose in Rachel's throat. She thought Papa was very adept—the two of them had done just fine before Miranda and Aunt Catherine arrived. She burned to tell him so, but since she couldn't contradict her elders, all she could do was sit in miserable silence while they discussed her fate.

Papa turned to Rachel, his brown eyes sympathetic. "Perhaps 'tis best, Rachel, that you not spend so much time with the Pugh children. Once you start school, I'm sure you'll quickly make other friends."

"Then I might see them sometimes, Papa?" Rachel tried to put into her voice the desperation she felt at having her friendships snatched away. If only she could make Papa understand.

Papa hesitated, and Rachel dared to hope. But then he shook his head. "I think not. 'Tis best to make a clean break. I shall see about your schooling tomorrow. That way you shan't have so much idle time."

A heavy blackness was closing in on Rachel. She wished Miranda and Aunt Catherine had never come. She asked to be excused and fled upstairs to her room.

Rachel flung herself onto her bed and lay there on her stomach, motionless. She was too angry to cry. She hated the way Miranda had swept into her life and started making it over, as if Rachel were a dress that had gone out of fashion. Rachel had been afraid a stepmother would change her life, but she had never dreamed it would start the very first day.

And how unfair to judge Sally and Todd because of what they wore and what their mother did for a living! Rachel dug her fingers into the crocheted coverlet. She couldn't believe Papa had allowed himself to be swayed by Miranda and Aunt Catherine's snobbery. Especially since he had remarked to Rachel several times that he admired Mistress Pugh's sharp business sense and the way she had kept the tavern prosperous even after her husband died.

Rachel rolled to her side and glared at the bed curtains. It wasn't right that she should never visit Sally again. What would Sally think when Rachel simply stopped coming to the tavern without a word of explanation? Rachel imagined Sally waiting for her day after day. Eventually Sally would be hurt, and angry. Maybe she would even hate Rachel.

Rachel couldn't bear the thought of Sally hating her.

For a while Rachel struggled over what to do. Then she made a decision. Even if it meant disobeying Papa, Rachel would go to the tavern and explain things to Sally. She put on her walking soles and grabbed her cloak from its hook on the wall. Then she slipped down the servants' stairway and out the back door.

Chapter 5
The Island

The evening was clear and cold, with a bright half-moon shining silver on the rooftops and on the ship masts in the harbor. Rachel pulled her cloak close around her. She had never been out alone at night. She was comfortable enough on quiet Church Street, lined with lit windows, but as she turned onto Tradd and walked toward the harbor, she grew more ill at ease. Most of the windows here were dark, and the few buildings that were lit seemed to be taverns, with knots of rough-looking people spilling out of the doorways and onto the sidewalk. Once, she passed a couple of sailors who turned their heads and leered at her as she went by. Rachel's heart beat faster until she was far past them and in sight of Mistress Pugh's tavern.

Quickly Rachel ducked inside, but she cringed by the door, put off by the noise inside. The taproom was smoky and dimly lit, and it was crowded with people, most of

them sailors, judging by their pigtails and baggy trousers.
The babble of voices was so loud Rachel wondered that
anyone could hear the person next to him. In the far corner, Rachel spotted Mistress Pugh handing tankards of ale
to a group of brutish-looking men with knives strapped
to their belts. Rachel didn't see Sally and Todd anywhere.
When Mistress Pugh finished serving the men, she came
over to Rachel and wrapped her arm around her. "What
brings you here this time of evening, love?"

Rachel longed to pour her heart out to Mistress Pugh.
But how could she tell Mistress Pugh that Papa consid-
ered her children unsuitable companions for his daughter?
"I've something important to tell Sally," Rachel said. "May
I see her?"

"Certainly," said Mistress Pugh. "She's upstairs preparing the room for our patrons for the night. Go on up, dear."

There were three rooms upstairs, two used by the Pugh
family and one rented out to guests. Rachel found Sally
changing bed linens in the guest room. She was singing
to herself, her back turned to Rachel. Rachel stood for a
moment in the doorway, feeling awkward, trying to think
how to bring up such an uncomfortable subject. There
was no easy way, she decided. She would simply have to
get on with it. "Sally," she said.

Sally jumped and whirled around with her hand on
her chest. "Rachel, you gave me such a start. What are
you doing here?"

"I came to tell you . . . well . . . that I shan't be coming to see you anymore."

"Why not?" Sally said.

Rachel plunged into her story. The tears that she hadn't been able to cry before now flowed freely. Sally handed her a handkerchief but didn't say a word as she talked. When Rachel finished, Sally still didn't say anything. She simply sat silently on the edge of the half-made bed.

Rachel had no idea what her friend was thinking. She began to wonder if she had been wrong to tell Sally the truth. Maybe she had been wrong to come here at all. Maybe it *would* have been better to have left everything alone, make a clean break, as Papa said. Why did it seem that Rachel always did and said the wrong things?

Finally Rachel could stand Sally's silence no longer. "Sally?" she said. "Are you angry?"

At first Sally didn't answer. Then she said, "No. 'Tisn't your fault what your elders do. I can't say I'm really so surprised. I might have known your stepmother would object to our friendship. The Pughs are not the sort of folk who'd be invited to dine with the governor, if you know what I mean."

Rachel hated to admit it, but she did know what Sally meant.

"'Tis the way things are," Sally said, "like it or not."

Something about the resignation in Sally's voice inflamed Rachel. "I don't like it," she said. "Not one bit."

She went and sat on the bed beside Sally. "Somehow we must find a way to go on being friends. We must."

"I wish there *was* a way," said Sally. "But I should hate for you to anger your father by coming here against his wishes."

"Then Papa mustn't know I've disobeyed him," said Rachel. "If only there were someplace we could go to talk where no one would notice us. Trouble is, Charles Town is so small, and your mother and my father are too well known here. Word would eventually get back to Papa of what I was doing."

"Then what we need is someplace outside of Charles Town," Sally said, her face lighting up. "And I know just where. There's an island, out beyond the mouth of the Ashley, where Papa used to go to fish. He took me with him one time, a few months before he died. I'm certain I could find it again."

"An island? How would we get there?"

"We'll row out in Papa's skiff. 'Tis still moored at Blount's Bridge and in good condition. The island isn't far offshore, and being on the Ashley side of the sound—'tis tricky to maneuver, y'know, and so swampy—no one ever goes there."

"I don't know, Sally. I've never rowed a boat before. And my clothes . . ." Rachel looked down at her silk bodice and matching overskirt. "How would I explain if I ruined my gown?"

"Don't concern yourself," Sally said brightly. "You'll wear a gown of mine. I have another. And only one of us need row, after all." Sally took Rachel's hands in hers. Her eyes were shining. "'Twill be great fun, Rachel. We shall explore the island, pretend to be pirates. What do you say?"

"I can't imagine myself tramping about on an island."

"Then don't try to imagine it. Just say you'll do it."

For a moment more Rachel hesitated. Then she broke out in a grin. "You're persuasive, that you are, Sally Pugh. How could I help but go along?"

"I knew you'd agree," said Sally. "But pray, don't breathe a word to Todd. You know he can't keep a secret, the way he rattles on."

Now that Rachel had warmed to the idea, she found her excitement growing. "Let's go tomorrow, then." She thought a minute. "I could probably sneak out after dinner. Aunt Catherine mentioned that she and Miranda always take an afternoon nap."

"Perfect," said Sally. "Afternoons are slow in the tavern. I'm certain Mama can spare me for a few hours."

The girls planned to meet in the tavern's stable at three o'clock and from there take backstreets to Blount's Bridge.

As Rachel was leaving, she thought again of the rough-looking men downstairs at the corner table and wondered aloud if they were the guests for whom Sally was preparing the room. "I should think 'twould be impossible to sleep with the likes of them across the hall," she said to Sally.

"Oh, they come here often," said Sally, "but they never stay the night. They're sailors. They sleep on their vessel." The overnight guests, she said, were a man and his wife who were boarding a ship tomorrow.

"I'm glad to hear it," Rachel said. "Those men are dreadful-looking. They remind me of the pirates who attacked our ship on my voyage here."

"I've heard it said they *are* pirates, but Mama doesn't like us to talk about them. They're some of her best customers, y'see. Pay their bills with gold coins. You see precious little of those in Charles Town, to be sure."

Then Sally edged nearer to Rachel and lowered her voice. "But between you and me, Rachel, they do scare me, especially the one man that usually comes in with them. He talks with an accent—he's a Spaniard, I think. His very voice makes me nervous, I tell you. And he has a beard as black as tar. Some folks say he's Blackbeard come to life again. He gives me gooseflesh, he does."

Rachel shivered as she remembered the cold stare of the pirate captain onboard the *Betsy Jo*. "The Spaniard . . . he's not downstairs now, is he?"

"No, I didn't see him," Sally replied.

"Thank heavens for that," Rachel said. "I never care to see another pirate as long as I live." Then she bade Sally good-bye and hurried downstairs and back through

the taproom, careful not to give so much as a glance to
the men at the corner table.

The next day, Rachel ate very little at the noon meal.
She was too excited and nervous about the coming adven-
ture with Sally. She nibbled at her rice pilau and waited
for everyone else to finish, which seemed to take forever.
At last Papa pushed away his plate and announced that he
was going to the docks to meet with some planters who
wanted to look over his ships. Aunt Catherine declared
that she and Miranda were going upstairs to nap, as was
the custom of well-bred ladies. This she said in Papa's
direction, but Rachel knew that it was meant for her.

"Perhaps I shall nap, too," Rachel said, opening
her mouth in a put-on yawn. "A nap can certainly be
rejuvenating." *If one needs rejuvenation,* she added silently.
Rachel definitely did not.

"Yes." Aunt Catherine smiled. "My sentiments exactly.
After our naps, we shall all be refreshed, and we'll take a
turn in the carriage before supper. Say, around five?"

Rachel smiled back, although weakly. She liked Aunt
Catherine, and she felt guilty for misleading her, though
she told herself she hadn't really lied. She had never said
she *would* take a nap, only that she *might*. It was merely a
trifling detail that she had no intention at all of doing so.

Rachel followed Aunt Catherine and Miranda upstairs. She waited in her room until she felt sure the two of them must be asleep. Then she took writing paper from her desk, dipped a quill in the ink pot, and jotted a quick note: *Could not sleep. Went for a walk. Pray go for your ride without me. I shall see you at supper.* She left the note propped against a candlestick on the desk.

That should give Rachel plenty of time. Supper was at seven.

Rachel put on a wide-brimmed straw hat over her linen cap and slipped her walking soles over her shoes. She had to look as if she were really going for a walk. She tiptoed across the landing and stepped on a loose floorboard, which creaked under her weight. The sound seemed to echo down the hall. Rachel prayed Aunt Catherine and Miranda were heavy sleepers. She glided down the staircase, and in the foyer at the bottom of the stairs she glanced at the grandfather clock by the front door. It was a quarter past three. She was late. She hoped Sally had not given up on her.

When she got to the stable, though, Sally was waiting with a dress for Rachel to change into, a simple calico with fitted sleeves and a pinafore. "I've outgrown it," Sally said. It was a little short on Rachel but much more comfortable than her fancy silks. The best of it was, she could shed the tight stays that always pinched her ribs.

Rachel hid her clothes in an empty stall but kept her

hat. "'Twill never do to come home with a sunburn," she said. Sally looked to make sure no one was in the court-yard—particularly Todd. "I saw Todd come out here earlier. I think he was looking for me." Seeing no one, the girls dashed out of the stable, only to run into Todd coming out of the necessary house.

Todd stared at Rachel, as if it took him a minute to recognize her. "'Tis you, Rachel! You look strange. You're wearing Sally's dress."

Rachel exchanged glances with Sally. Now they were in for it. How were they going to explain why Rachel was wearing Sally's clothes?

"She's trying it on for size," Sally said. "Now run along into the house."

"Mama said you and Rachel were going somewhere. I want to come, too."

"Not this time," Sally said.

Rachel bent to Todd's level. "'Twould give you no amusement, Todd. We're planning to talk, mostly. Of girlish, trifling things." She made as sour a face as she could muster.

"Why don't you take your canoe out to Oyster Point and go clamming?" Sally suggested.

"Why can't I come with you?" Todd begged.

"Because you're too little!" Sally snapped. "Away with you! Leave us be."

Todd looked as if he was about to cry. With shoulders

drooping, he turned and trudged back to the house. The girls watched him disappear inside.

"Poor thing," Rachel said. "Weren't you a mite harsh with him, Sally?"

"Did you want him to come along?" Sally asked. Her voice was hard, but Rachel saw tears glistening in her eyes.

"No," Rachel said quietly.

"Then let's be going." Sally was already heading for the courtyard gate.

It wasn't far to Blount's Bridge. The skiff was over-turned onshore with the oars stored underneath. Todd's canoe was beside it. Before Rachel knew it, she and Sally were skimming through the sound on their way to the island. The sun glittered golden on the water and fell like warm buttermilk on Rachel's arms and face. The oars made a gurgling sound as they stirred up suckholes in the skiff's wake.

The clean salt smell of the sea came to Rachel's nostrils even as the island itself was only a dark line of forest on the horizon. Rachel took over the oars for a while. Rowing was easier than she had thought it would be. Then the marsh came into view, its grasses waving in the breeze. The wide, sweeping marsh teemed with birds, and their notes filled the air. As the skiff approached, a long-legged bird fishing on a sandbar squawked and mounted to the sky. A pair of spotted birds that Sally called sandpipers flitted along the island's bank, searching for mussels in the salty mud.

"'Tis low tide," Sally commented. The water was so shallow, it was useless to row. Instead Rachel used the oar to push against the mud and propel the skiff toward the mouth of a tidal creek that formed a sheltered cove amid the tangle of trees. A large, black-and-white bird of prey took off from its nest in a dead tree at the edge of the creek. Rachel watched as the bird wheeled into the air, then plunged into the marsh after a fish. Rachel couldn't take her eyes off the magnificent hunter, even as it sailed with its dinner into the sky.

Which is why, at first, Rachel didn't see the rock. Sally did, and she pointed it out to Rachel. It was a large, smooth stone, perfectly round, sitting in the salt mud in the middle of the creek's mouth. Most of the stone was a dark gray and covered with scattered deposits of coral and barnacles, but the top was a much lighter color and free of deposits, as if it alone was uncovered at high tide. On the dark part of the stone, about two feet below what must have been the waterline, there seemed to be a figure cut into the rock.

The girls pulled the skiff onto the bank and waded out into the mud to have a closer look. The figure was in the shape of an upside-down pear. Rachel thought it was very mysterious. "It looks," she said, "like a symbol of some kind."

"It must be a symbol," said Sally. "See, 'tis etched into the rock." She traced the marking with her finger. "The rest of the stone is perfectly smooth."

Rachel rubbed her own fingers over the indentations. "What do you think it means?"

"I don't know. Carved by Indians years ago, I'd think. Yamassees once lived all around here. 'Course, they've been gone now some thirty years. Perhaps this stone marked the island as a favorite for hunting or fishing."

"Then why would they place it *here*," Rachel said, "where the tide would cover it up?"

Sally shrugged. "Who knows? Maybe they wanted to keep it a secret from other tribes. You'd fairly have to be looking for it to find it—you'd have to come only at low tide, y'see."

Rachel thought Sally's guess made sense. Then a troubling thought occurred to her. "Sally," she said very slowly, "you don't suppose that *pirates* cut this symbol, do you? That they use this island to hide their plunder and don't want the marker to be seen?"

Sally shook her head. "'Tisn't likely. The island's too close to Charles Town. Pirates are more careful than that, else their necks would be in a noose. I'm thinking the island was an Indian haunt. Why don't we look around a bit? Perhaps we'll find some arrowheads. Then we'll know for certain."

Rachel agreed, though she reminded Sally they didn't have much time. The girls made their way into the dense forest, following the creek as it wound and twisted through the tangle of trees and the spreading ferns and shrubs. The banks of the creek were steep, overgrown with grass and reeds and littered with stumps. As the girls walked by, turtle after turtle slid from the slippery mud and plopped into the black water. Here and there were water snakes, gliding along the surface or sunning themselves on logs or tree roots. Once, off in the forest, Rachel spied the quick white flash and instant motion that was a white-tailed deer. Everywhere was the roar of insects, the whine of mosquitoes.

The creek forked near a clump of sweet-smelling bushes. The larger branch of the creek flowed on into the forest, while the lesser branch twisted through the shrubs. The girls would have taken the larger branch except for the rattlesnake that lay coiled in their path. It lifted its mean little head and shook its rattle, a sound barely louder than the whir of an insect but plenty loud to warn the girls away.

So they took the smaller branch. It led them on for a few hundred yards through briars and plants with scratchy, fanlike leaves, but it gradually diminished, then trickled away into a swampy area surrounded by a thick grove of tall, fragrant shrubs profuse with leaves, which Sally called wax myrtle bushes. Here the earth sucked at the girls' feet as they walked. In one place, solid ground gave way suddenly to greasy mud, and a little way beyond, a black, gaping sinkhole. Even from where she stood, Rachel could smell the foul odor of the sinkhole, the smell of dead and rotting things. It nearly overpowered even the sweet-smelling myrtle.

"We'd better not go any farther," Sally said. "'Twould be too easy to slip and fall into that sinkhole."

"'Tis an evil-looking thing," Rachel said, staring at the sinkhole. "How deep do you think it is?"

"Could be knee-deep." Sally shrugged. "Could be bottomless. I shouldn't want to find out."

"Neither should I," said Rachel. Then she bent to examine a chiseled rock she had just noticed sticking halfway out of the mud. "What's this?"

Sally came closer. "It looks like an arrowhead," she said with excitement. "I wager I was right about the Yamassees. What a perfect hunting ground this would be. The myrtle's leaves are so thick and full, the Indians could have hidden here to ambush their prey—deer, most likely—and if the poor thing ran, it'd fall slap in the sinkhole and be stuck fast. Then the hunters would pull it out and have venison for dinner."

Rachel tried to imagine Yamassee hunters of years ago crouching among the shrubs with their bows and arrows.

The nearly impenetrable grove would certainly make a good hiding place, she decided.

Sally suggested they look around for more arrowheads. "I'd love to bring some home to Todd. He's fascinated by Indians. 'Twould be a sort of peace offering," she said brightly.

With very little effort the girls found several more. Rachel also found something she would rather have not. She spied a trace of white protruding from some leaf litter and, thinking it was an arrowhead, reached to pick it up. At her touch the leaves fell away and Rachel saw, to her horror, the grisly grin of a human skull. It was all she could do to stifle a scream.

"Probably some hapless hunter who fell in the sinkhole," Sally said.

It took Rachel a while to recover from her scare. Then the girls started back to the cove. They had just reached the fork of the creek when Rachel noticed a splotch of white against the dark of the trees ahead. She jumped back in alarm when suddenly the splotch exploded into a whir of flapping wings, and a great white bird lifted up through the canopy of leaves and disappeared. "What was that?" Rachel exclaimed.

Sally laughed. "A snowy egret. They're supposed to be good omens. 'Tis strange, though, to see one so far back in the woods. Perhaps 'twill bring us luck."

"It already has," Rachel said. She was eyeing something

on the trunk of the pine tree where the egret had been perched. It was the same pear-shaped symbol that they had seen before, this time carved into the soft wood of the pine.

But the exposed wood was white, not at all grayed from age. There was no way the symbol could have been cut more than a year before, if even that—which meant there was no way that Indians could have made it. Rachel's pulse began to beat faster.

If Indians hadn't made these symbols, then who had?

CHAPTER 6
A DISCOVERY

Rachel pointed out the symbol to Sally. "You know what I think?" said Rachel. "I think the symbols were meant to mark a trail, to lead somebody somewhere on the island."

"You mean like a map?"

"Yes, though I can't imagine to what the trail would lead. There doesn't seem to be a great deal of anything on this island. Except snakes. And mosquitoes." Rachel slapped at a large black mosquito perched on her wrist.

"I know," said Sally, slapping at a mosquito on the back of her neck. "Yet 'tis a big island. Perhaps we'll find something the next time we come."

Rachel felt a tiny quiver of misgiving. Somehow she couldn't quite get pirates out of her mind. "What exactly do you expect to find, Sally?"

"Oh, I don't know," Sally said. "Probably nothing. 'Tis thrilling, though, to *think* about finding something."

Rachel agreed. It *was* exciting to think about discovering something on a deserted island, a little like Robinson Crusoe. Yet though Rachel didn't want to admit it to Sally, a part of her hoped that all they did was *think* about it, that they would never really find anything.

Sally noticed then that the tree frogs had started to sing, which meant dusk was nearing. Following the creek, the girls hurried the short distance back to the cove. The tide had started to come in, and the symbol on the rock was already covered.

As the girls slid the skiff back into the water, Sally suggested they give the island a name. "Though it mustn't be just any old name," she said, climbing into the boat. "It should be something fitting."

"Something exciting and a bit mysterious," Rachel added. She handed Sally the oars and climbed into the bow of the boat herself. "Something that would truly describe it."

"Well," said Sally. She was starting to row. "The symbols were exciting and very mysterious. But the skull was mysterious, too." She paused. "I think we should call the place Skull Island. What say you?"

"Yes. Skull Island." As Rachel spoke the words, a breeze kicked up. The water rippled and goose bumps prickled across her arms. Rachel hugged herself and shivered deliciously.

Skull Island.

It was a perfect name. And Rachel couldn't wait to come back.

⟡

As it turned out, though, Rachel did have to wait. At supper Papa informed her that the next day she would begin lessons with Madame Varnod, a widow who lived on King Street and operated a school for girls out of her home. Apparently, Rachel was the last to find out. Miranda and Aunt Catherine seemed to know all about the arrangements.

"You'll be learning all sorts of needlework, Rachel," said Miranda, "as well as drawing and French."

"A perfect education for a young lady," said Aunt Catherine.

Both of them seemed very pleased, but Rachel was sick with disappointment. How long would it be before she had another chance to see Sally and go back to the island?

Early the next morning—Wednesday—Rachel trudged dutifully up Church Street and two blocks over to the narrow single house occupied by Madame Varnod. She and her husband were among the flood of Huguenot refugees who had come to Charles Town from France to escape religious persecution. Madame spoke French more reliably than she did English, and she peppered her instruction with so many French phrases that Rachel, who knew no

French at all, had to struggle to understand the least thing that Madame said to her.

What was worse, spring had sprung all over Charles Town, and nowhere more so than in Madame's garden. The schoolroom overlooked the garden, and Rachel's eyes were constantly drawn to the window. Several small, spreading trees were golden with blossoms. Bumblebees hummed over borders of lilies and poppies. Roses and flowering vines climbed Madame's garden wall, and every breeze bore their sweet scent. Rachel chafed at being stuck inside doing embroidery and lacework and learning French phrases. She daydreamed all day about Skull Island and the strange symbols—who made them, and what they meant.

It was out of Rachel's way to go home by the tavern, but she went anyway. She *had* to see Sally and plan when they might go back to the island. They decided to go on Saturday afternoon, after Sally's chores were finished and Miranda and Aunt Catherine lay down for their naps.

Never had two days seemed so long. It was only the thought of going back and exploring the island that got Rachel through.

On Saturday morning Rachel awoke to the warmth of sunlight on her face. For a moment she lazed in bed, reluctant to get up and face the hours at Madame Varnod's. Then she remembered what day it was. Her eyes flew open and she jumped out of bed. She need not sew a single

stitch today, nor speak a word of French. Today she and
Sally were going to Skull Island!

Rachel went to the window, threw up the sash, and
looked out across Charles Town. There was the spire of
Saint Philip's, the bells just beginning to peal the hour.
Rachel listened to the chimes as they came. *One-two-
three-four-five-six-seven.* Over the tiled housetops, Rachel
could see the tall masts of ships in the harbor. Had it
really been only a month ago that she had arrived in that
very harbor? She breathed deeply, sucking in the delicious
salt air. How she loved the smells, the sights, the sounds
of Charles Town! Why, today she even felt charitable
toward Miranda. Rachel had to admit that Miranda's
being here seemed to make Papa happy.

Rachel headed downstairs for breakfast. Papa was
standing at the mirror in the foyer, straightening his wig.
He was already dressed for work, Rachel saw, in a purple
waistcoat and breeches. "Leaving before breakfast, Papa?"

"Good morning, my dear." Papa kissed the top of
Rachel's head. "I have some early business at the ware-
house. And of course I'm coming home early to escort
Miranda and Aunt Catherine to the Manigaults' ball
this evening."

Rachel had forgotten about the ball. The Manigaults
were close friends of Papa's and were giving the ball in
honor of his engagement.

It couldn't have come on a better day, Rachel thought

with delight. Miranda and Aunt Catherine would be busy all afternoon getting ready—having their hair dressed and powdered and their faces made up. Rachel couldn't help smiling as she thought about how easy it would be to slip away to meet Sally and go to the island.

"And is my absence at breakfast so pleasing to you, daughter?" Papa teased.

"Oh, no, Papa," Rachel said. "I was thinking of something else. Of course I'll miss you at breakfast."

"A likely story," he said, smiling. Then his tone turned serious. "How are you getting along in school, Rachel?"

"Fine, I suppose." Rachel would never dare tell him that she was bored to death.

"Are you making friends?"

Rachel didn't know what to say. She really had talked very little to the other girls at school. Their greatest concern seemed to be the latest fashions in London and Paris, and since clothes didn't interest Rachel, she had kept pretty much to herself. "I know I shall eventually, Papa."

"You will. I'm certain of it." Papa laid a hand on her shoulder. "It may take some time, but 'tis for the best, truly." Rachel knew he was referring to his ban on her friendship with Sally and Todd. Papa just assumed she'd obeyed him and ended the friendship. Rachel's conscience tweaked her, but only slightly.

Then he went on. "Miranda only has your welfare in mind, Rachel. I want you to remember that. She's much wiser about these things than I. Which brings something else to mind. She also suggested I enroll you in dancing lessons, and I have done so. You'll begin next Saturday afternoon at two with Master Holte on Meeting Street. If you learn quickly, perhaps we shall take you with us the next time we attend a ball."

Dancing school! Was it Miranda's plan to fill Rachel's every waking hour with lessons? Miranda was determined, wasn't she, to make Rachel into a proper lady, whether Rachel wanted to be one or not.

But Rachel knew she had no say in the matter. Papa's word was law. She was only glad that Papa had made arrangements for next Saturday, rather than today. At least she could still go to the island with Sally.

Rachel looked up at Papa and smiled. "Yes, sir, that would be lovely. Good-bye, Papa." As Papa went out the door, Rachel glanced at the grandfather clock beside the door. Nearly half past seven. Only six more hours until she could leave for Sally's, six and a half until she could slip into the comfort of Sally's cotton gown and they could be on their way. Six hours would pass quickly, Rachel was sure. She skipped into the dining room for breakfast.

On the island, Rachel and Sally moored their boat in the mouth of the creek and tramped eagerly into the woods, searching for more of the carved symbols. They followed the creek as it snaked through the forest, but veered away from the creek when they found another of the symbols on a tree, beside a deer trail that twisted through the woods and up a densely wooded hill. As the girls followed the trail up and up, the trees became a thick, pressing curtain around them. Then the ground leveled off, and in the distance Rachel heard the sound of thunder. A knot of uneasiness formed in her stomach. She suggested to Sally that they turn back. "I should hate to be caught in a storm in so eerie a place," she admitted.

"Don't worry," said Sally. "'Tis only the breakers. We must be nearing the ocean." A few minutes later they rounded a curve in the trail and nearly ran smack into a huge, perfectly round boulder, half as tall as Rachel.

Cut into the top of the boulder, larger than they had ever seen it before, was the carved symbol. It was impossible to miss, and so unexpected that for a moment Rachel could do nothing but stare. Sally must have been equally surprised. She was standing with her mouth hanging open.

But as Rachel stared at the rock, she was struck by the impression that it reminded her of something, something beating around in the back of her mind that she couldn't quite catch. Then it came to her, a memory from her days aboard the *Betsy Jo*: the ship's crew throwing overboard large round rocks to lighten the *Betsy Jo*'s load when they wanted to increase her speed. Ballast stones, the rocks were called.

Rachel's mind raced. If this rock was a ballast stone—and it made sense that it was—it was brought to the island by sailors, sailors who then went to a lot of trouble to carry the stone across the island, put it here in the middle of this path, and mark it with the symbol. Rachel breathlessly told Sally what she was thinking.

"Of course!" said Sally. "After all, this stone and the one in the cove are really the only large stones we've seen on the island. Yes, they were put here on purpose, Rachel, to mark something, where someone who knew what to look for could easily find them. But what were they meant to mark?"

"The beginning and the end of the trail, perhaps?"

"What else could it be?" wondered Sally. "Though it doesn't look as if the trail has led to much, does it?" She pointed a few yards beyond the boulder to the top of a ridge, where the trees opened up into daylight and the earth ended abruptly in blue sky. "Unless there's something at the bottom of that ridge," Sally added.

"There *must* be something," Rachel said. Her earlier qualms about what they might find were forgotten. Tingling with excitement, she rushed to the crest of the ridge and peered over. She found herself looking down a steep grade that dropped into a water-filled basin—a saltwater pond. On three sides, wooded ridges loomed above it, and on the fourth, a great, rolling sand dune. Behind the dune, the surf roared. At high tide, the pond was probably much wider and deeper, but now, at low tide, it was scarcely more than a large tidal pool edged by a ribbon of salt mud and reeds.

"A hidden lagoon." Sally had come up beside Rachel.

"Mmmm." Rachel only half-heard Sally. She was staring hard at something in the middle of the lagoon, a dark pyramid shape protruding from the greenish-black water. She could barely see it through the glare of the late-afternoon sun. "Sally, what is that?" she said, pointing.

Sally squinted. "It looks like a pile of stones."

Rachel's heart began to pound. "Ballast stones?"

"Aye, I think so." Sally's voice brimmed with excitement. "Do you think *that's* what someone was meant to find?"

Rachel chewed on her lip, thinking. "If it is, I can't imagine why—unless something is hidden under the stones." She gazed down the slope, strewn with fallen logs and overgrown with briars and creeping vines. "Shall we try to get down there and have a look?"

"Not if you're to be home for supper. Look at the sun."

Rachel glanced over her shoulder at the sky. The sun was balanced just over the top of the trees behind her, and the day's warmth was already ebbing. It *was* getting late, Rachel had to admit, but she burned with curiosity about that pile of stones. With her dance lessons beginning next Saturday, who knew whether she would ever have another chance to come back and investigate? "Come, Sally. It won't take long. Just one quick look." Rachel started forward over a rotten log.

"Rachel!" Sally grabbed the sash of Rachel's apron and pulled her back. "Come to your senses, will you? We barely have time to get across the island before dusk. We have to go *now*."

Rachel was a little put off by Sally's bossing, but once they were in the woods, Rachel had to admit that it was a good thing they'd started back. Under the heavy canopy of trees, the woods were murky gray. Sunlight was fading, and the trunks of the oaks quickly grew dense with shadow, their mossy beards stirring eerily in the half-light. Dusk crept through the forest like a living thing. Rachel heard the noises of its coming—the evening birds' flutey notes, the croaks of frogs, the distant call of a whippoor-will—and she felt its deepening chill. She couldn't have been more glad when at last she and Sally burst from the dark shadows to the golden light of the marsh.

But then they both gasped. There in the mouth of the creek, right beside their skiff, was Todd's canoe!

CHAPTER 7
LOST IN THE FOREST

"Todd followed us!" Rachel exclaimed.

"I should have known," Sally said. "Todd can't abide being told he can't do something. How shall we ever find him before sunset? And him afraid of the dark." Her face was pained.

"We'll find him," Rachel said, determined not to let her own fear show. She couldn't bear the thought of Todd alone at night in that forest.

The girls hurried back into the woods, where the shadows were quickly giving way to a gloom so thick that Rachel felt she could reach out and touch it. They searched desperately for Todd, calling and calling his name until they were both hoarse, yet all that answered them was silence.

Rachel scarcely noticed the hordes of mosquitoes that whined around her head, or the rustling and scurrying of the night creatures in the bushes at her feet. A terrible, cold sickness had begun to grow in her belly. *What if they didn't find Todd?*

Then, curling out of the darkness, came Todd's cry: "Help me!"

"Todd, where are you?" Sally called.

"Help me!" It sounded fainter.

"Tell us where you *are,* Todd!" Sally yelled frantically.

A feeble "Help!" was all that came back.

Sally turned to Rachel and wailed, "Dear Lord, Rachel, he's hurt, I know it. If anything happens to him, I shall never forgive myself."

Rachel fought against her own rising panic. Willing herself to stay calm, she put an arm around Sally. "We'll follow the sound of his voice. We'll find him, Sally." Then she yelled, "Todd! Keep talking to us! Keep calling for help!"

Rachel waited for his answer. Silently she pleaded, *For once in your life, Todd, do what you're asked. Please.* She waited for decades, it seemed. Then, at last, came the most welcome sound Rachel had ever heard: "Yes, Rachel." Todd's voice was very weak. "Help. Help. Help."

"Louder, Todd," Rachel yelled. "Louder!" She was desperately trying to determine from which direction his voice was coming.

"Help! Help! Help!"

"This way!" Sally said. She bounded forward like a bloodhound on a scent, pushing easily through a tangle of shrubs. Rachel was right behind her. They followed the sound of Todd's voice, until Rachel began to think the area looked familiar. Then she caught the unmistakable scent of myrtle, and she knew where they were. They must be on the other side of the myrtle grove. *Near the sinkhole.*

Suddenly Rachel knew what had happened. The area around the sinkhole was full of arrowheads. And Todd was fascinated by Indians . . .

Sally, her voice stricken, put into words what Rachel was thinking. "He's fallen in the sinkhole! Oh, Rachel, I hope we can get him out."

Rachel didn't answer. She was afraid her voice might give away the terror she was feeling. She kept seeing in her mind that hideous skull and hearing Sally say, *Probably some hapless hunter who fell in the sinkhole . . .*

Without a word, Rachel grabbed Sally's arm and plunged through the myrtle bushes. She felt the ground go springy under her feet, and she made herself slow down and take careful, measured steps. She motioned for Sally to do the same. Then Rachel saw him. Todd was mired to the waist in mud, clinging to a root that jutted out into the sinkhole. Even in the waning light, Rachel could see his arms shaking.

"Hold tight, Todd," Rachel said. "Just a few minutes more." Her eyes were sweeping the clearing for a sturdy branch that was long enough to reach out to Todd.

"The mud is sucking on me," Todd said. His voice trembled. "It won't let me go." His arms tensed as he made an effort to pull himself out.

Rachel saw him slip a few inches deeper into the mud. Sally rushed past Rachel to the edge of the sinkhole and dropped to her knees. "Toddy, be as still as a mouse. The more you struggle, the more you'll sink."

"Yes, Sally," Todd said weakly. His arms relaxed.

Rachel had found a sturdy pine branch. She lay on her belly and stretched it out over the mud. "Grab on, Todd."

"With one hand, Toddy," Sally said. "Keep hold of the root with the other."

Todd slowly stretched out one arm toward Rachel, as if he was afraid to move a muscle. His fingertips fell inches short of the tip of the branch.

"I can't reach," he whimpered.

"I'll get it closer to you, Todd," Rachel said. "Sally, hold on to my feet." Sally grabbed Rachel's ankles, and Rachel slid forward on her belly until her chest extended out over the mud. Her heart thudded. The putrid smell of the mud filled her nostrils. She tried not to think about what would happen to her if Todd pulled too hard on the branch. "Can you reach it now, Todd?"

Todd looked ghostly pale in the waning light. Rachel held her breath as his fingers wormed toward the branch, then latched on. "Yes! Yes, I have it!" he exclaimed.

"Hold on tight, then," said Rachel. "We'll have you out straightaway."

"Don't you dare let go," Sally said.

Slowly Rachel rose to her knees and then to her feet, pulling, but the mud clutched Todd firmly in its grasp. Rachel broke out in a cold sweat. What on earth would they do if they couldn't get Todd out? She braced herself and tugged harder, but still the mud clung to him.

Now Sally was beside Rachel, helping. Rachel felt the mud give just a little. "He's coming!" Rachel cried. She pulled with all her might. Sally strained and grunted with effort, and, little by little, Todd began to emerge from the mire: first his waist, then his hips and his thighs, and finally, with a greedy *sluurrpp,* the mud released him. Todd was free!

They collapsed, all three, in relief and exhaustion. Todd seemed unhurt, but now darkness covered the forest like a shroud. Not a single star nor the light of the moon penetrated the gloom. It was so dark they couldn't even find the creek. They started back, or the way they thought was back, but after a while they felt themselves going uphill, and they knew they were lost.

"We must be headed up the side of the ridge," Sally guessed.

"Perhaps we can find the boulder," Rachel said. "Then we'll know where we are and can follow the deer trail back to the creek and the creek back to the boats."

"Even if we could find the boulder," Sally said, "—and that's doubtful—I don't think we could see well enough to follow the deer trail. Remember how side trails veered off from it right and left? We could end up more lost than we are right now. Or one of us could fall into another sink-hole, or step on a rattlesnake, or trip and break a leg."

"Or get eaten by a panther," Todd threw in.

Rachel sighed. "You're right. 'Tis too risky to be tramping about in the dark. So what are we to do? Spend the night here in the forest?" Even as she said it, Rachel felt a shiver skitter down her spine. She thought she would rather take her chances with a panther.

"'Tis our only choice," Sally said. "Let's go further up the ridge, where the trees are sparse. Perhaps there will be enough moonlight that we can see a little. Then we can look for shelter and try to get some sleep."

The three made their way up the ridge and found, when they broke through the trees, that there wasn't any moon and, since the night was cloudy, very few stars. They could see only dimly, but the girls thought they were prob-ably near the top of the ridge that overlooked the lagoon. They found some thick shrubs and huddled underneath, for a cold breeze was blowing on the ridge, and Todd had started to shiver.

Under the shrubs' drooping branches, it was fairly warm—at least bearable—and, before long, Todd was sound asleep. Soon afterward, Sally's slow, even breathing

told Rachel that she also had dropped off. Though Rachel
ached with weariness, her worries wouldn't let her sleep.
What dire consequences would she face when she got
back to Charles Town tomorrow? She had broken so many
rules, and broken Papa's trust as well. He was sure to be
dreadfully angry. Perhaps, Rachel worried, he would be
so angry that he would send her back to New York. The
thoughts went round and round in her head and would
not stop.

Sometime, though, Rachel must have fallen asleep, for
the next thing she knew, she had jerked awake. Something
had awakened her—voices, she thought. She strained to
listen but heard nothing. Maybe she had only dreamed
it. Her eyelids drooped, and she felt herself drifting off.
Then, suddenly, she heard it again, distinctly—the rumble
of voices, not too far away. Rachel's eyes popped open.
Her every sense was alert.

"Sally," Rachel hissed. She nudged Sally's shoulder.
"Wake up. There's someone here. Someone else is on
the island."

"I'm already awake," whispered Sally. "I heard the
voices, too. They're somewhere below us."

"Oh, Sally." Butterflies fluttered in Rachel's stomach.
"The voices must be from down in the lagoon. Perhaps
the sailors who left the stones have come back."

"What sailors?" asked Todd, just waking up. His
words rang through the stillness, and Rachel stiffened.

If we can hear them way down there, she thought, *can they hear us up here?*

"Ssshh, Todd. 'Tis nothing," Sally whispered. "Go back to sleep."

"If 'tis nothing," Todd boomed in a defiant tone, "why must I be quiet?"

Todd's stubbornness was going to be their ruin! Rachel took a deep breath to calm herself, then said quietly to Todd, "We thought we heard voices from the bottom of the ridge. We think someone's down there."

"Let's go down and see who it is," said Todd. His voice was animated, though at least now he was whispering.

Rachel's heart pounded. She didn't dare mention to Sally and Todd the awful thought that had jumped to her mind: that the sailors were pirates, come to the island to . . . to . . . what? Rachel didn't know *what,* since Sally had said the island was too close to Charles Town for pirates to bury their treasure. Pirates! Perhaps it made no sense to think such a thing, but she couldn't help what was in her mind, could she?

"Oh, no," Rachel said, "we dare not. Whoever they are, they may be . . . dangerous."

"'Tis likely they are," said Sally. "But perhaps we could see from the ridge what they're up to." She glanced at the sky. "The stars are actually quite bright now that the clouds have cleared."

Rachel looked up and saw that the sky was peppered with huge silver stars, so bright that they cast a net of light over the entire landscape, even though there was no moon. The children crept to the edge of the ridge, lay on their bellies, and looked down.

A light was bobbing about in the lagoon—a lantern. In its glow, Rachel could see two men—one big and stout, one tall and slender with a dark beard—wading into the water.

The big man had on dark knee breeches, a waistcoat and a short coat, and heavy boots. The slender man wore a ruffled white shirt and baggy breeches tucked into thigh-high boots. Both men had on wide-brimmed hats that obscured their faces.

They didn't look like any sailors Rachel had ever seen . . . or pirates, for that matter. But it certainly appeared that they knew about the ballast stones. They were headed straight for them, slogging through the knee-deep water. The big man was holding the lantern, talking loudly to his companion—or talking at him, for the slender man didn't appear to be answering. Rachel strained to hear, but she could only make out a few phrases, something about goods and getting paid. When the men reached the pile of stones, they stopped. The slender man finally said something, but Rachel could not understand the words. She looked quizzically at Sally. "He's not speaking English," Rachel whispered.

"I think it is English," Sally responded. "But with a Spanish accent."

"Aye," Todd said, "he sounds like the Spaniard who comes in the tavern. You know, Sally, your favorite customer."

Then angry voices from the lagoon pulled Rachel's attention there. The two men were arguing, but then they must have decided something, for they stopped arguing abruptly, and the slender man, cursing, started unpiling the ballast stones.

Rachel's pulse quickened. She knew it! There *was* something underneath the stones! For a moment, excitement overrode her fear as she watched the slender man lift off stone after stone. Sally and Todd were like statues as they, too, watched.

After what seemed like forever, the slender man stopped, reached inside the pile, and pulled out a small barrel. He pried off the lid and lifted out a box, which he handed to the big man. Then he put the empty barrel back and re-piled the stones around it, and the two men began to make their way to shore.

"I wager there's treasure in that box," Todd whispered. "Spanish doubloons!"

There. Todd had said it, or almost said it. Treasure . . . Spanish doubloons . . . that meant pirates. And from what Rachel had seen in the last few minutes, the idea that the men were pirates didn't seem so far-fetched anymore.

"Enough of your fancies, Todd," Sally snapped.

But Rachel said gravely, "I don't believe 'tis but a fancy to think the men pirates, Sally."

Sally didn't answer, and it occurred to Rachel that perhaps the idea of pirates had been in Sally's mind, too, and she was trying hard not to heed it.

All Rachel wanted now was for the men to take their box and get off the island—fast. But as soon as the men waded ashore, she realized they had no intention of hurrying. The big man planted himself on a log, with the box in his lap. The slender man stood beside him, looking over his shoulder. For a while their attention was riveted on whatever was inside the box. Then the big man handed something to the slender man, and the slender man burst into a rage. He let out a string of angry words that had to be curses, and before Rachel knew it, he was lunging at the big man. The big man seemed to go berserk. He jumped on his companion and started pummeling him with his fists. Rachel saw the flash of a knife and heard a scream.

Rachel felt as if she were caught in a nightmare. Was a man to be killed before her very eyes?

CHAPTER 8
RUINED

The last thing Rachel wanted to do was watch the scene below her, but she seemed to have lost the ability to move. She couldn't even turn her head to look at Todd and Sally, though she heard them beside her, breathing hard, and somewhere in her brain it registered that they were as frightened as she was.

Then, suddenly, like a white squall whose fury was spent, it was all over. The slender man was still alive. The big man had yanked him to his feet and held him locked in a vise grip. The slender man muttered something in his thick accent, and the big man growled, so loudly Rachel could hear every word: "If you ever betray me again, my friend, I *will* kill you, make no mistake about it."

Such a shiver went down Rachel's spine that it chilled her to her very bones. All at once she had the overwhelming feeling that the big man could somehow see her and Todd and Sally on the ridge. She felt herself begin to shake.

She turned to Sally and mumbled, "We should quit this place *now.*" She didn't dare speak the words that hung in her head: *Before they come after us.*

Quickly the three of them scrambled down the ridge and back into the woods. The only thought in Rachel's mind was to find a place to hide. When they did find a place, in the hollow of an ancient oak, they huddled there for a long time, listening, terrified that the men would take the marked deer trail back through the woods and that the trail might be somewhere nearby. All they heard, though, were the night noises of the forest—the croak of tree frogs, the singing of crickets, the hooting of owls.

It must have been in the wee hours of the morning when Todd finally dropped off to sleep, then Sally. But Rachel didn't sleep at all. Every time she shut her eyes, she saw again the scene in the lagoon, and, try as she would, she could not rid her mind of the fearful ring of the big man's voice.

From her hiding place, Rachel watched the forest ease toward dawn. The black went to indigo, and the indigo to gray, and the trees gradually took shape. Rachel figured it was light enough now to see their way back to the cove, so she woke Sally and Todd. Silently, cautiously, they made their way through the woods, watching and listening lest the men they'd seen last night were still on the island. But the men were apparently gone.

They reached the cove safely, and the marsh stretched

out before them like a vast silver shield. A single seabird winged across the sky, though a multitude of birds sang from the grasses that rippled in the barest breeze. Across the water, the dark line of trees on the mainland glowed faintly pink.

Once they were in the boats—Todd in the canoe and the girls in the skiff—they talked at last about what they had witnessed in the lagoon. They all agreed the men must be pirates.

"Just think," Todd said, "we're the only folks on earth who know where pirates bury their treasure. 'Tis ours for the taking. We'll be rich, Sally. I shall never again have to muck out the stables." He was almost singing as he lifted and dropped his paddle into the water.

"We shan't be rich," Sally said, with a powerful pull on the skiff's oars, "because we're not coming back."

"Why? Are you scared?" Todd's tone was taunting.

Sally's eyes flashed. "You bet your grandfather's wig I'm scared, and you should be, too. Pirates are cutthroats, Todd. They're not to be trifled with. There are plenty of other islands around Charles Town. I've had quite my fill of this one, thank you."

Rachel heartily agreed. She planned never to set foot on Skull Island again.

Saint Philip's clock was chiming six when Rachel, Sally, and Todd slipped through the tavern gate and into the stable so that Rachel could change her clothes. The tavern was still dark, the roosters just beginning to crow. "We can climb the trellis and slip right in our bedroom window," Todd suggested. "Mama will never know a thing."

"Todd, think," Sally said a bit impatiently. "Mama's likely been worried to death. We shall have to tell her everything. I'm sure she'll forgive us, though, when she hears what we've been through."

As Rachel started home, she had no such hopes for forgiveness. She walked slowly down Tradd Street and turned onto Church. What had happened last night when she didn't come home for supper? And what would happen this morning when she presented herself after being gone all night?

What possible excuse could she make for her absence? She could think of none. And the truth . . . oh, the truth would make Papa so angry Rachel shuddered to think of it.

It was Sunday morning, and most of the households on Church Street were not yet stirring. In front of one house a small black boy was out sweeping the steps. Her own house was dark. Soundlessly, Rachel slipped through the front door—residents of Charles Town never locked their houses at night—and up the staircase into her room. She stripped to her chemise and climbed into bed. Despite her worries, before she knew it, she had dropped into an exhausted sleep.

Rachel was awakened much later by a rapping at her door. "Miss Rachel." It was Adele, one of the maids. "Your breakfast is ready."

Rachel shook her head, trying to dislodge the grogginess that clung to her brain. Adele was calling her to breakfast, just as usual on Sunday morning. For a moment Rachel wondered if she was still asleep, and dreaming. But no, there was an ache in her neck where she'd slept on it wrong, and she felt the warmth of the sun even through the drawn bed curtains. It was certainly very peculiar. "As if I had never been gone," Rachel whispered.

Adele was still knocking at the door. "Miss Rachel? Your papa and Miss Miranda are waiting at table."

"I'm coming, Adele," Rachel answered. She jumped out of bed and washed and dressed hurriedly. What was afoot? Was Papa to dole out her punishment at breakfast in front of Miranda? *That would be bitter to swallow,* she thought. As she went downstairs to the dining room, Rachel tried to prepare herself as best she could to face Papa's anger.

To Rachel's great surprise, Papa smiled at her as she took her place at the table. As soon as Rachel sat down, the kitchen maids began serving breakfast—fresh flounder and hominy grits. "Good morning, daughter," Papa said. "I trust you slept well."

Rachel looked at Papa, blinked, and nodded. She felt her mouth hanging open and made an effort to close it. Then she glanced, perplexed, at Miranda, who was also smiling, and at Aunt Catherine's empty chair. *What was indeed afoot?*

Miranda must have misunderstood Rachel's baffled expression and thought Rachel was wondering about Aunt Catherine. "Aunt Catherine was exhausted from the ball," she said. "We didn't want to wake her this morning."

"I'm afraid the late night may have been too much for her," Papa said with concern.

"I hope Aunt isn't taking ill," Miranda said. "I understand Mistress Brownlow went to bed feeling indisposed yesterday afternoon."

"Yes, but she's better this morning," said Papa between bites of flounder. "She wouldn't allow me to send for Doctor Trent."

Rachel's thoughts all but burst from her. *Mistress Brownlow had gone to bed sick, and with Papa, Aunt Catherine, and Miranda at the ball, no one had even missed Rachel yesterday.* Rachel couldn't believe her good fortune. She suddenly realized she was very hungry.

For the next few days, Rachel didn't dare sneak away to see Sally and Todd. She tried hard to attend to her

lessons at Madame Varnod's and to do everything that
Mistress Brownlow told her. Rachel took walks with
Aunt Catherine—purposely avoiding looking down Tradd
Street toward the Pughs' tavern—and tried not to be
jealous when Miranda and Aunt Catherine retired into
the parlor with Papa every evening, leaving Rachel to
study her French alone in her room.

One evening, though, Rachel decided she couldn't
stand it any longer. She simply *had* to visit Sally and see
what had happened to her friends after Saturday night.
Papa was in the parlor, as usual, with Miranda and Aunt
Catherine. Leaving her French book open on her desk,
Rachel grabbed her straw hat and went downstairs. At
the bottom of the stairs she paused, listening to the lively
voices coming from the parlor. Rachel recalled the cozy
evenings she and Papa had spent together before Miranda
came. She wondered whether Papa missed their evenings
together as much as she did.

Probably not, Rachel thought. *He has Miranda to keep
him company now.*

Just then, Papa's laughter rang out from the parlor,
deep and hearty, and Miranda's light, feminine laughter
followed. Loneliness welled up inside Rachel. She felt she
couldn't bear to stay here and listen a second longer. She
pushed herself out the front door and on to the tavern.

Rachel went straight around back to the tavern
kitchen. Sally did most of the cooking in the evenings,

and Prudence and Mistress Pugh served the customers. The tavern courtyard was dark, but Rachel knew her way by heart.

She walked along the brick walkway past the garden and saw Sally through the lighted kitchen window, sitting in front of the hearth, stirring something in an iron cauldron. Todd was chopping vegetables at the pine table. From out of the kitchen drifted the delicious aromas of stew and baking biscuits and the sweet smell of burning bayberry candles. The light from the fire flickered on Sally's face, and Rachel could almost feel the warmth of the hearth. Rachel's loneliness eased. She lifted the latch of the door and went in.

Sally turned at the sound of the door, and her eyes lit up in genuine pleasure. "Well, good evening to you, Rachel Howell. I thought you'd forgotten us."

"Rachel wouldn't forget us," Todd said. "Here, have a carrot." He handed Rachel the stub of carrot he'd been chopping, the last one remaining. "Now I'm through, Sally." He set down the cleaver and wiped his hands on the seat of his breeches.

Rachel, chuckling, took a bite of the carrot. "I see you're just using me, Todd, for your own devices."

"I am not!" Todd said indignantly, then, in a thoughtful tone, added, "What are devices?"

Sally shook her head indulgently. "Rachel's teasing you, Toddy." Then to Rachel she said, "We have missed you, though. We were worried that your father was angry with you for Saturday night."

Rachel explained how she hadn't even had to account for her absence. "How about you?" she asked. "Was your mother very angry?"

"Angry as a hornet!" Todd exclaimed.

"She wasn't," Sally insisted. "Not really. She was vexed for sure . . . at Todd for running off, and at me and you for not telling her when we first discovered the symbols on the island. But mostly she was relieved that we were safe."

"Mama thinks the men we saw were pirates," Todd said, his eyes shining. "And she said we're never to go back to the island, nor tell a soul what we saw, lest the pirates come after us and run us through with their swords!"

"Todd!" Sally scolded. "You know you're exaggerating. Mama didn't say a word about the pirates' swords." She rolled her eyes. "What she *said* was that the men likely *were* pirates, and she didn't want us returning to the island. And I was glad to promise it, I tell you the truth!"

"Tell Rachel about the Spaniard," Todd begged.

"Oh, yes, how could I forget that?" Sally chided herself.

Rachel looked at Sally with interest. "The Spaniard?"

Sally started to explain. "Well, you remember my telling you about the Spaniard who comes into the tavern, the one folks say is Blackbeard come to life again?"

Rachel nodded, and Sally went on. "He came into the tavern Sunday morning—we weren't even open—and,

Rachel, *he asked my mother to tend a knife wound on his face.*"
These last words she spoke slowly, with great intensity.

At first Rachel didn't understand the significance, but
then it struck her. "Oh, my word. Your Spaniard is the
same man we saw on the island!"

Sally nodded emphatically.

"He wouldn't let Mama send for a surgeon, either,"
Todd added. "Which is proof enough he's a pirate, if you
ask me."

Sally's eyes flashed. "You'd best watch your tongue,
Todd. Mama warned you how serious it is to accuse someone of piracy, without a shred of proof. A person could be
hanged for being a pirate; you know that. For once, you'd
better mind Mama. Do you hear?"

Rachel thought Mistress Pugh must have really given
Todd a talking-to, for he sobered immediately and promised
not to do it again.

"Will you have some stew?" Sally offered. She was
ladling spoonfuls of golden-brown stew into wooden
bowls.

"I gathered the oysters myself," Todd said proudly.

Even though Rachel had already eaten, her mouth
watered at the sight of the chunks of oysters swimming
in thick vegetable broth. It smelled heavenly. "Perhaps
a quick bowl," she said.

Rachel gobbled the stew, then took her leave. She
hurried up Tradd and turned onto Church Street, only

to stop short within sight of her own house. An elegant
carriage hitched to a team of six beautiful grays waited on
the street in front of her house, the driver, in green livery,
still aloft the driver's seat. A footman, also in green, stood
on the sidewalk. It was odd enough that someone would
come visiting this time of night, but odder still that such
a fine carriage wasn't taken around to the carriage house.
Whoever had come to call must be in a huge hurry, not
expecting to stay but a moment—which most likely meant
he or she brought news of an urgent nature, news that
couldn't wait until morning.

Rachel rushed up the street and slipped through the
gate into the courtyard. The parlor curtains had not yet
been drawn, and Rachel could see Papa in the parlor, his
back turned, talking to someone, a gentleman. But shadows covered the man's face, and Rachel couldn't see who
it was. Miranda, Rachel saw, was sitting in the wing chair
by the fireplace, and Aunt Catherine was on the settee.
While Rachel watched, Miranda stood up and grasped
the corner of the mantel, as if she needed support. The
light from the sconce above the mantel fell square on her
face, and she looked so pale that it frightened Rachel.
What terrible news could Miranda be hearing?

Rachel hastened around the corner of the house, not
even mindful of the click of her heels on the flagstone
walkway. Across the veranda and through the back door
she went, her mind so fixed on what was happening in the

parlor that she nearly ran right over Mistress Brownlow. The housekeeper was standing in the hall, feather duster in hand but her ear pressed to the parlor's closed double doors. Rachel could hear heavy voices drifting through the doors. One voice she recognized as Papa's, and the other she thought she recognized, too, though she couldn't place it.

"Miss Howell!" Mistress Brownlow shrilled. "Young ladies of your station do not run down hallways, if you please!" Rachel figured Mistress Brownlow was more put out about being caught eavesdropping than about Rachel's running. The way the housekeeper stood, waving her feather duster and flapping her bony arms, made Rachel think of a bat startled from its perch. Rachel might have laughed if she hadn't been so worried.

"I'm sorry, Mistress Brownlow," Rachel said. "I was in a rush to see Papa." Rachel's mind raced. Somehow she had to get past Mistress Brownlow and into the parlor to find out what was going on. Or did she? After all, Mistress Brownlow *had* been listening at the door, and no one loved showing off what she knew more than Mistress Brownlow did.

Rachel's brain was churning. "Do you think Papa would mind," she began, "if I interrupted his chat with the parson? I had something quite important to tell him."

Mistress Brownlow raised her chin and sniffed. "'Tis not the parson to whom your father is talking. 'Tis his business partner, Mr. Craven. And I'm certain he doesn't wish to be disturbed."

Mr. Craven! Rachel thought. If *he* came bearing bad news, it must have something to do with Papa's business venture in Barbados. Hadn't Papa said he had invested a great deal of money in that venture?

Rachel felt a pressure building in her chest. "What are they speaking of?" she asked Mistress Brownlow.

"I'm sure I don't know," Mistress Brownlow said grandly. "I make it a point to mind my own business, young lady, and you should do the same. So off with you."

At that moment, though, the parlor doors flew open, and Papa strode into the hall. His face was drawn and gray, his jaw clenched. It spurred an image buried deep in Rachel's memory: Papa sitting like stone at her mother's funeral, while only she, closest to him on the hard church pew, saw the lone tear slide down his cheek. Rachel felt a stab of pain for her papa, then and now.

"What's wrong, Papa?" she said to him.

Papa looked at her sharply, as if he had just noticed she was there. "I'm going away, Rachel. There's a ship in the harbor now bound for Philadelphia at first light. I must be aboard."

Rachel went cold. "Why?" she asked. "Why must you leave?"

"I have a friend there I must see . . . see if he can loan me money."

"But you have money aplenty, Papa." It popped out before Rachel had even thought about it. But surely it was true.

"Not anymore." Papa's eyes looked so hopeless that Rachel felt like crying. "Our ships from Barbados were captured by pirates," he said. "We've lost everything. We're ruined now, Rachel, unless I can secure this loan." He kissed her on the head. "Be good, my dear. I'll write you when I arrive in Philadelphia. Now I must pack and get down to that ship." Then he rushed past her and up the stairs.

CHAPTER 9
GIFTS

Rachel felt cold all over, as if a stiff ocean breeze were blowing right through the house. She couldn't take her eyes off the landing where Papa had disappeared into his bedroom. She was aware of Mistress Brownlow feverishly swishing the feather duster along the banister. From inside the parlor, Rachel heard a woeful "Oh dear, oh dear, oh dear." Aunt Catherine. In answer came the voice Rachel had thought she recognized earlier, which she now knew as Mr. Craven's. He sounded impatient. "Come now, madame. 'Tis not as bad as all that."

Aunt Catherine rushed out of the room, dabbing her eyes with a handkerchief. She swept past Rachel and up the stairs without seeming to notice her.

A wave of distaste for Craven flooded Rachel, more pronounced than she had ever felt before. *Easy for him to say,* Rachel thought bitterly. *He hasn't lost everything, has he?*

Rachel made herself turn to look in Craven's direction. He was standing beside Miranda at the mantel, talking to her in a low voice. Miranda seemed to be listening very intently and then, to Rachel's surprise, she smiled tremulously. It struck Rachel as totally out of place with the situation.

What on earth had Craven said to her?

Rachel watched Craven take Miranda's hand and kiss it, just as he had on the night of their first meeting, though she distinctly noticed that Miranda did not cringe this time.

But Rachel didn't have time to think about it, for she heard her papa's footsteps on the stairs and felt the rush of air as he hurried down. Soon he would be on his way to Philadelphia, and Rachel would be left here with Miranda and Aunt Catherine. She yearned to throw her arms around him and beg him to take her along. But, of course, she couldn't do that.

"Good-bye, Papa," she said, barely above a whisper.

"Good-bye, lamb." Papa kissed her again. Then he added, tenderly, "I shall be home before you know it."

All Rachel could do was nod. She didn't dare look at him; her eyes were swimming with tears, and she didn't want him to see.

Papa must have said good-bye to Miranda, but Rachel didn't remember it. Her last impression of Papa was of his calling to Mr. Craven, who was to drop him

at the docks. Then Papa was out the door, and Craven
was strutting past Rachel, and Miranda was standing
in the parlor doorway with a mournful expression on
her face.

A disturbing question flickered through Rachel's
mind: Whose departure was Miranda sad about?
Papa's . . . or Mr. Craven's?

Over the next few days, Rachel went several times
to the tavern to talk to Sally, but each time the taproom
was packed with customers and Mistress Pugh said she
couldn't spare Sally from the kitchen. Rachel thought
perhaps Mistress Pugh blamed her for putting her children in danger on Skull Island. And no wonder, Rachel
told herself. She shuddered every time she thought
about what might have happened and what a narrow
escape they had had. Ever since Papa left, Rachel had
had nightmares about the big man chasing her, calling
through the dark forest that he would kill her if she
ever betrayed him.

In her waking hours, Rachel worried about Papa
constantly and wondered whether he had arrived yet
in Philadelphia and how long it would take a letter
from Philadelphia to make its way to Charles Town.
Toward the end of the second week, Rachel began to

hope that she might hear from Papa any day, but still no letter came.

By now it was mid-April, and Rachel learned how fickle South Carolina springtimes could be. The weather turned unseasonably cold, and a chill wind blew from the sea. The azalea blossoms froze, turned brown, and fell off the trees. It rained every night, and every morning Rachel walked to school through a dreary gray mist. By noon, though, the sun had burned off the mist and warmed the air, and Rachel always shed her cloak on the way home from school.

Lately Rachel had taken to walking home by way of Bay Street, even though it was a bit out of her way, so she could stop at the wharf to see if any ships had arrived with news from Papa. On this particular afternoon, Rachel had just turned from Tradd onto Bay when she saw something that gave her such a start she instinctively jumped into the alley next to the cooper shop she had just passed. Coming up Bay Street was Miranda, arm in arm with Craven!

Rachel's mind rocked. *Papa said Mr. Craven is a recluse, rarely seen on the streets of Charles Town—yet here he is, strolling along with Papa's fiancée. And Papa gone!*

Rachel tried to convince herself it could all be innocent. Perhaps Mr. Craven was simply being kind, showing Miranda around, helping her fill the time so she wouldn't miss Papa too much.

Mr. Craven being kind? Rachel shook her head. *Not likely.* She peered around the corner of the building to see what he and Miranda were up to.

They had stopped in front of Mr. Stevenson's dry-goods store. They were looking in the window, talking and laughing. Miranda was tilting her head from side to side and touching the straw hat she was wearing, apparently using the window as a mirror. She tied and retied the bright green ribbon on the hat. The hat must have been new, for Rachel had never seen it before. Craven was smiling and admiring Miranda in the hat. Even from where she stood, Rachel could hear him boom, "'Tis very becoming, my dear." Again Rachel felt sharp dislike for Craven.

Had Craven bought Miranda that hat? Rachel was sure of it. She sank down onto some barrels stacked in the alley. Craven buying gifts for Papa's fiancée—it just wasn't proper, especially not with Papa away. How could Miranda even think of accepting Craven's attentions?

Then Rachel remembered the way Miranda had smiled at Craven the night Papa left. Rachel felt sick. She had never really wanted Papa to marry Miranda, but she certainly didn't want to see him suffer the humiliation of having his fiancée stolen away by his own business partner. Yet what could Rachel do?

Rachel brooded over it all the way home. Finally she decided to tell Miranda what she had seen. She would do it at supper tonight. Only Miranda and Rachel would be there, for Aunt Catherine was dining out with friends. Maybe Miranda would come to her senses, would return the hat to Craven and stop seeing him altogether. Rachel could only hope so.

☙

Rachel stayed in her room all afternoon, rehearsing what she would say to Miranda, full of dread for the moment, yet eager to get it over with.

At last Saint Philip's bells chimed the supper hour: seven o'clock. Rachel went down a little late, hoping Miranda would already be at the table, but she wasn't. The dining room sideboard was spread with a fish pie and cold marinated beef, and the maids were bringing in platters of spiced crabs and steaming rice. Since Aunt Catherine was dining out, Miranda's place had been set at the head of the table and Rachel's to her right.

As Rachel seated herself, she realized that Miranda had been given Papa's chair, the seat of greatest honor. Staring at her plate, Rachel muttered, "I shall *never* feel that way about *her.*"

"Were you talking to me, Rachel?" Miranda had entered without Rachel noticing.

Rachel was flooded with panic. Had Miranda heard

what she said? "N-no," Rachel stammered. "I was talking to myself." She didn't raise her head.

"*I* used to do that when I was young," said Miranda cheerily. "I too was an only child." She pulled out her chair and sat down. "It sometimes becomes lonely, does it not?"

It was then that Rachel looked up, and she felt as if she'd been kicked in the stomach.

Miranda was wearing Rachel's pearl pendant!

Chapter 10
The Mansion on Elizabeth Street

For a shocked moment, Rachel could only stare at the pendant lying like a tear-shaped moon against Miranda's throat. Then Rachel's brain began to work, to turn slowly through her stupor. *It can't be my necklace. Papa must have had one just like it made for Miranda . . . But why would he do that? How could he not know how that would hurt me, after my necklace was lost to pirates?*

That her papa would be so unfeeling cut Rachel deeply. Her only thought was to get away from Miranda and from this room that suddenly seemed alien to her. "Excuse me. I don't feel well," she murmured, pushing away from the table. Somehow she made herself rise. The door, beyond Miranda, was miles away.

Miranda had risen also. "Rachel! Are you ill? Can I help you?"

Rachel began to walk. She was beside Miranda now.

As Miranda spoke, Rachel's eyes turned to her. All she could see was that necklace, identical to hers—the milky white pendant in the middle, the delicate seed pearls along the necklace's length, gradually becoming smaller and smaller . . . Then Rachel stopped, stared again. At the top of the necklace, near the clasp, one pearl was broken in half.

This necklace wasn't identical to hers. It was *hers!*

Rachel's heart started a wild drumbeat. "Where did you get that necklace?" The voice that came out of Rachel's throat was raspy and strange-sounding, as if it belonged to someone else.

Miranda's face clouded. It occurred to Rachel how rude her question was, but she didn't care. She thought she had a right to know. She waited for Miranda's response.

Miranda tilted her chin in the air. "It was a gift," she said crisply.

"From whom?"

The silence in the room was heavy and cold as ice. Rachel could hear the grandfather clock ticking in the hallway. Finally Miranda said, "I don't think 'tis your place, Rachel, to ask me that."

Rachel didn't hesitate an instant. "It is my place," she declared, "because I think 'tis my mother's string of pearls, stolen from me by pirates on my voyage here."

For a fleeting moment Miranda's face went white. Then it darkened. "That's absurd," she snapped. "How could they possibly be the same pearls?"

"I don't know," Rachel said. "But they *are* the same. Mine had a broken pearl near the clasp. On the left side. Go ahead. Feel yours."

Miranda's chest rose and fell with her breathing, rose and fell. Slowly she lifted her hand, touched it to the necklace, and let her fingers climb to the broken pearl. Rachel saw her eyes widen, heard her quick intake of breath as she felt the pearl.

Then Miranda's face became hard. "I know what you're trying to do, Rachel," she said, her voice harsh. "You're trying to drive a wedge between your father and me. You've never liked the idea of our marriage. You saw the broken pearl when you walked by, and you made up a story to upset me. I never would have thought you could be so wicked."

Rachel was stunned. At first she couldn't say a word, but then her temper flared. "Is it I who's wicked," she spit out, "or you? All you care about is my father's money, and you waste no time in jilting him when you think his fortune is gone!"

Rachel bolted from the room. She flew upstairs to her bedroom and slammed the door. Moments later she heard Miranda come upstairs. Rachel thought perhaps she was coming to apologize, but Miranda walked right past her door. Rachel thought she caught the sound of a muffled sob.

Remorse began creeping over Rachel. She had never spoken such hateful words to anyone. And what would

Papa say when he heard of Rachel's behavior? He'd be deeply disappointed, Rachel knew, and probably ashamed. Rachel didn't think she could bear Papa's being ashamed of her. She would have to apologize to Miranda.

When Rachel opened her door, though, to go to Miranda's room, she saw Miranda halfway down the hall, whisking toward the stairs, her shoulders straight and high in a determined posture. She had on her cape and the new hat. Her skirts swished as she swept down the stairs. She stopped in front of the mirror at the bottom of the stairs to straighten her hat, then called to Adele. "I may be late, Adele. Please tell Aunt Catherine when she comes home."

"But, Miss Miranda, your aunt took the carriage."

"I shan't be needing the carriage," Miranda said briskly, and she was out the door.

Where was Miranda going in such a hurry, and on foot? To meet Craven? Rachel made an instant decision: she would follow Miranda and find out. She whirled and headed for the servants' stairway that led to the back veranda. She raced down the stairs, through the dark courtyard, and out the gate, then stopped to see which way Miranda had gone. Though the night was cloudy, there was a bright half-moon, and it frosted the housetops with light.

Rachel saw Miranda about a block up Church Street in front of the Lawrences' house, headed north toward Cumberland Street. Rachel followed her, careful to keep a good distance between them. A damp night breeze was blowing, and Rachel wished she'd had the foresight to bring her own cloak.

Rachel trailed Miranda block after block to a part of town where the houses were very well-to-do, much more so than the Howells' residence. Miranda stopped in front of a lavish mansion on Elizabeth Street. It was surrounded by a low brick wall and was set back from the street beyond a wide lawn. Rachel went as close as she dared. She waited within a recessed gateway on the other side of the street, out of Miranda's sight.

At first Miranda only stood by the brick wall and looked at the mansion. Then her shoulders heaved—a sigh, perhaps?—and she went through the gate, across the lawn, and up the stairs to the veranda. She paused a moment, then lifted the heavy brass knocker and rapped on the door. Light spilled out as the door was opened. Rachel saw a black houseboy in the doorway. She crept up and crouched behind the brick wall to better see and hear what went on. She was conscious of her own breathing and the beat of her pulse in her throat.

Who would Miranda ask for? Craven?

What Rachel heard sent her mind reeling.

"Is my father home?" Miranda asked.

"He's in his library, Miss Miranda," the boy answered.

"I must see him at once." Miranda pressed past the boy into the house, and the door closed behind her.

Miranda's father in Charles Town! Rachel could scarcely believe her ears. Wasn't it strange that Miranda had never mentioned him? Rachel had always assumed Miranda's father was dead, for whenever Miranda spoke of her childhood, she talked only of her mother—and Rachel clearly remembered Papa telling her once that all Miranda's family, except for Aunt Catherine, lived in Philadelphia. Why would Papa tell Rachel that if it weren't true?

Maybe Papa doesn't know Miranda's father lives in Charles Town! Rachel thought. *Maybe Miranda has kept it from him. But why?*

All of a sudden the answer sprang, dark and enormous, into Rachel's head. Miranda wouldn't be likely to tell her fiancé about a father she believed to be a scoundrel. And that's what Rachel had heard Miranda call Mr. Craven the day they were introduced!

Could it be possible that Miranda was Mr. Craven's daughter? It would certainly explain a lot. Yet Rachel knew she was leaping to conclusions by making such an assumption. She needed to know for certain who lived in the house. For a while Rachel lingered outside, hoping a servant whom she could ask would come out, or perhaps even Mr. Craven himself.

Soon it started raining, first a drizzle, then a downpour. The downpour didn't last long, but Rachel, without her cloak, was drenched and cold. She had no choice but to go home. At her own house on Church Street, she managed to slip in the back door and up the steps without being seen, but even after she was warm and dry in bed, she couldn't fall asleep. Much later Rachel heard Miranda come in, and much, much later Rachel finally dropped off to sleep.

Rachel awoke with questions in her mind burning even more intensely than they had last night. She was eager to get back to Elizabeth Street and find out who lived in that house. At Madame Varnod's, she simply could not concentrate, so she told the widow she was ill and had to go home. Then she headed to the tavern to pick up Sally and Todd.

All morning the children watched the mansion from across the street, but there was no sign of life. No one drew the heavy drapes at the windows or unlocked the driveway gate. Not a soul ventured outside. At last Todd began to get restless. "No one's home," he said. "Let's go."

"It *don't* appear that anyone's home," Sally said. "I think the owner has left town. The house seems locked up tight."

"No," Rachel said, "I *know* he was here last night. Papa said Craven was a recluse. Perhaps he wants to discourage visitors."

"He's doing a right smart job of it then," said Todd, plopping himself down on some stairs leading from a walled courtyard.

"It seems that *someone* would come out," said Sally, "if only a maid to sweep the steps." She nodded her head toward the house next door to the mansion, where a skinny black slave-girl with rings in her ears was sweeping the veranda.

Rachel thought of Mistress Brownlow, who always seemed to know the neighbors' gossip. "Perhaps that girl will tell us who lives here," Rachel said. She marched through the neighbor's gate and up the stairs to the veranda. "If you please," she said, "my friends and I are not sure we have the right address. Would the house next door be the home of Mr. Craven, the shipping merchant?"

"Yes, miss, that's right," the girl said.

"Why is his house all locked up," Rachel asked, "as if no one lived there?"

"Oh, 'tis always so. He's a queer sort, that one," she said, "though don't go saying it was me who told you so."

"Queer in what way?"

"Comes and goes at odd hours, he does, scarcely shows his face in the light of day. Don't keep servants long, either. Why, he's had more housekeepers than I can count on my fingers. And that's just in the three years since I've been here."

"How long has he lived there? Do you know?"

"Oh, years, miss, years. Now I must get back inside. I've the washing to do."

Rachel thanked the girl and went back to Sally and

Todd. She told them what she had learned. "It makes me furious to think that Miranda's been deceiving Papa all this time." Rachel's voice was heavy with bitterness.

"She may have her reasons," Sally said softly. "As you do, for deceiving your papa about your friendship with us."

Rachel felt the blood rush to her face. She'd never looked at her friendship with Sally as a *deception*. After all, it wasn't as if she had set out to lie to Papa . . .

"'Tisn't the same," Rachel said. "Papa's forbidding our friendship wasn't reasonable. 'Twasn't even his idea. 'Twas Miranda's."

"*I* don't think Craven *is* her father." Todd stood up suddenly. "Why, they haven't even the same last name."

"Oh, he's her father, to be sure," Rachel said. "I heard her call him such."

"Perhaps one or the other of them changed their name," said Sally.

"Yes," said Rachel. "The question is who . . . and why." She paused, screwed up her face, and ran her finger absently along the brick wall beside them. "I'm inclined to think 'twas Craven, for Miranda seemed not to recognize his name when Papa first mentioned it." She went on to tell her friends everything that had happened the afternoon Miranda arrived, including the conversation Rachel overheard between Craven and Miranda.

Sally shook her head. "'Tis a wonder anyone could feel such contempt for her own father as to call him a scoundrel. Whatever he did must be prodigious bad."

"You would think so, would you not?" said Rachel. "And you'd think 'twould be hard for her to put those feelings aside. Yet now it seems she has. Suddenly he's her beloved papa again, showering her with gifts."

"And them both hiding it from your father," said Sally.

"I wager," said Todd, "'twas *Craven* who gave Miranda your necklace, Rachel!"

Rachel was startled. Todd had put into words what had been in the back of her mind since last night: somehow Craven had gotten his hands on Rachel's necklace and had given it to Miranda. Rachel had thought it too preposterous to consider before—how *could* Craven have gotten the necklace?—but now that the idea had been spoken aloud, it sounded almost logical.

Rachel's heart began to race. "The pendant *was* unusual," she said. "Craven likely thought such a distinctive present would win Miranda back to him for good."

"Perhaps Miranda was as shocked as you to find the pearls were yours," Sally said.

Rachel thought about that as she watched a carriage roll past them down the street. "That *would* explain why Miranda was so upset. She realized her father had given her a stolen necklace, and she was worried about how he had gotten it."

"So how *did* he get it?" Todd asked. He had seated himself on the stairs again.

"That's what I don't understand." Now Rachel was shaking her head.

"He could have bought it here in town," Sally said. "Mama says certain Charles Town merchants will buy cargo off any ship, even suspicious cargo, no questions asked, if they can get it cheaply enough. Then they sell the goods in their shops for far less than the honest merchants charge. And they still make huge profits. She says it goes on all the time."

"What an easy way to get rich," Todd commented.

"Is it not illegal, though, to buy goods from pirates?" Rachel asked.

"Of course," said Sally. "I suppose they figure the money they make is worth the risk."

Rachel narrowed her eyes. "You really think Craven might have innocently bought my necklace from a shop in town?"

"'Tis possible," Sally said, hesitating a little, "but from what you've told us of him, I think 'twould be more likely that *he* was the dishonest merchant buying from pirates."

Craven buying from pirates . . . an easy way to get rich . . . Suddenly everything made sense to Rachel—Craven's expensive attire, his fine carriage and lavish home, her instinctive dislike of the man. Excitement ran through Rachel like rushing water. "Of course," she said. "It fits Craven perfectly. Now I understand why he didn't seem as concerned as Papa about losing all that money when their ships were plundered."

"Aye," said Todd. "He's making his fortune buying from pirates."

But Sally's face had clouded. "You know, Rachel," she said, "I just had a terrible thought. If Craven *is* dealing with pirates and gets caught, your father, as his business partner, could come under suspicion. And the penalty for dealing with pirates . . . well . . ." She cast her eyes down and wouldn't look at Rachel. "'Tis the same as if one were a pirate himself."

Rachel stared in horror at Sally. She'd heard enough to know what happened to pirates. *Papa would be locked in the guardhouse and made to stand trial. Then, if he were convicted . . . the gallows.*

CHAPTER II
TROUBLE FOR PAPA

Rachel's head pounded. *She couldn't let that happen to Papa.*

"Then I must find out whether 'tis true what we think about Craven," she said. "And tell Papa as soon as he comes home, make him believe me somehow." She sighed and rubbed the ache in her temple. "Though I've no idea how to do so. Or where to begin."

"Begin with Miranda," Sally suggested. "See what you can learn from her."

"Yes," said Rachel, with a thrust of her chin. "I shall begin with Miranda."

Rachel went home right away. She found Aunt Catherine doing needlework in the parlor. Rachel asked her if she had seen Miranda. The old lady didn't answer, only looked queerly at Rachel over her spectacles.

Rachel squirmed. Had she forgotten to wash her face this morning? Why was Aunt Catherine staring at her so?

Finally Aunt Catherine pushed up her spectacles and spoke in a serious tone. "What brings you home so early, Rachel? Has Madame Varnod taken ill?"

The time! Rachel groaned and cast a quick look at the clock in the hallway. It was only half past twelve. She'd been so caught up in her purpose she had completely forgotten that she wasn't due home for more than an hour. How was she to explain?

Before she could think, Rachel heard herself answer. "No, Aunt," she said. "'Twas I who wasn't feeling well. I just need to rest a bit, I think. I'll go right up." Rachel could hardly believe the lie had come so effortlessly. It made her feel wretched. She backed away before Aunt Catherine could question her further. Then, as if it were an afterthought, she asked again, "Is . . . Miranda home?"

"Yes, Miranda's upstairs in her room. Are you certain you'll be fine?"

"Oh, quite," Rachel said. "I may take a nap. No need to call me to eat."

Rachel made herself walk leisurely up the stairs, though she really wanted to run. She was anxious to see what she could learn from Miranda. The door to Miranda's bedroom was closed, and Rachel knocked, but there was no answer. She knocked again, more loudly. When there was still no answer, Rachel cracked the door slightly.

"Miranda?" she called.

No answer.

Rachel opened the door all the way and peered inside. Miranda was not in the room, and her walking soles, which she kept by the door, were not there. That meant Miranda had most likely gone out, without telling Aunt Catherine.

Rachel's eyes swept the room. An overturned book lay on the arm of Miranda's settee. Rachel also saw something stuffed under the settee's cushion. Curious, she went over and plucked it out. It was Miranda's new straw hat, or at least what was left of it. The hat had a hole through the middle, and part of the brim was torn away. The ribbon had been pulled out entirely. *What had happened to the hat?* Rachel wondered.

Then, on the floor beside the settee, Rachel noticed a sheet of folded writing paper, sealed with a drop of wax, though the seal had been broken. Lines of fancy script covered the page.

Rachel's pulse thudded. She knew with dead certainty that something in this letter had been the cause of Miranda's sudden outing. Dare Rachel read it?

For a long moment she struggled with her conscience. Then, telling herself that reading the letter was in Papa's best interest, Rachel picked up the paper and scanned what was written on it. Today's date was at the top of the page. Below the date, Rachel read:

My darling,

Our argument last night greatly distressed me, as you know. I rejoice that it may yet have a happy resolution should you decide to accept my proposition. Yes, my dear, I was serious; I do not think you realized how serious. I trust, now that you have had time to reflect calmly on our discussion, you will agree to join me. If you still desire to decline, a note to that effect will suffice. But if, as I hope, you accept, please come here at your earliest convenience and we will discuss the particulars.

The letter was not signed, but Rachel didn't need to guess who it was from: Craven. Bitterness rose in Rachel's throat. *Miranda had wasted no time in rushing off to accept that snake's proposition.*

Now Rachel was more worried than ever. Craven and Miranda keeping secrets from Papa, plotting together behind his back, with him away—surely it meant trouble for Papa, deep trouble. Somehow Rachel had to find out what Craven and Miranda were up to. A sense of haste gripped her. She would go immediately and tell Sally and Todd about the letter. Together they would think of something. They had to.

Rachel set the letter down. She quietly stepped into the hallway, intending to slip out of the house by the servants' stairs, but before her hand had left the doorknob, she saw that Aunt Catherine had just come up the front staircase and turned into the hallway. Rachel knew there was no hope of sneaking out now.

"Oh, Rachel," Aunt Catherine said. "I was just coming up to look in on you. Did you talk to Miranda?"

"Uh—no," Rachel stammered. "She was asleep." Rachel wasn't sure why she lied; why should she make excuses for Miranda? Then an idea came to her—a way she could get out of the house. It was another lie, and Rachel was disgusted at the easy way it slid out of her mouth. "You know, Aunt Catherine, I changed my mind about napping. I think it's fresh air I need. A turn about the courtyard, perhaps. Or even a walk."

"If you please, dear. Did you see the letter from your father on your chest of drawers? It came this morning. I forgot to tell you about it."

The long-awaited letter from Papa! Rachel thanked Aunt Catherine and rushed to her room. She snatched the letter from the chest and eagerly broke open the seal. The letter had been sent more than a week before from Philadelphia. Rachel's eyes flew across the lines, but, as she read, a tightness pulled harder and harder around her chest.

> *I am sorry to tell you, daughter, that I have been unable to secure the loan. Thus, our financial future looks bleak. In view of the circumstances, lamb, it may be best for you to return to your grandparents' home in*

New York. As painful as the separation would be for both of us, your grandparents could provide for you properly, as I am no longer able to do.

Rachel couldn't read any farther. She felt her misery would swallow her alive. Papa meant to send her back to New York. Didn't he know she'd be just as happy—happier—living like Sally, as long as she was with him?

Then her thoughts took another disturbing turn. Papa would have written a similar letter to Miranda, Rachel guessed, telling *her* of his misfortune. *That* was why Miranda had been so eager to accept Craven's proposition! She'd forgotten Papa in an instant and rushed out to see to her own interests. Rachel's stomach knotted in anger. "Like father, like daughter," she said to herself. "I don't trust either of them."

Rachel's temple was throbbing again. Rubbing it, she returned to Papa's letter. In the last line he wrote that he would already be on his way home by the time she received the letter. If winds held steady, he said, his ship should arrive in Charles Town on the thirteenth of May.

This was May ninth. Papa would be home in only four days!

Rachel had looked forward so long to his return, but how could she be happy now? Everything looked so bleak. Papa was penniless. He would soon be sending her back to New York, and something sinister was going on between his business partner and his fiancée. There was nothing Rachel could do about Papa's fortune, or his decision to send her to her grandparents. But at least she could try to find out what Craven and Miranda were up to, though she didn't have much time.

Rachel hurried to the tavern and went straight to the kitchen, where she knew she would find Sally and Todd. She told them about Craven's proposition and Miranda's involvement, Papa's letter and his imminent return.

Sally waited until Rachel finished, and then she spoke up quickly. "Did you ever think you might be jumping to conclusions, Rachel, about Craven and Miranda? The man's her father, after all. His proposition to Miranda may have nothing at all to do with his business, or with your papa."

"But I don't trust Craven," Rachel rushed on. "I haven't from the first." Rachel thought briefly about the few times she'd seen Craven and the uncomfortable way he made her feel. "Something about him has always made me wary, though I'm not certain what . . ." Her voice trailed off.

"'Tis his eye, I wager," Todd said.

Rachel shook her head. She was struggling to identify something tugging at her memory.

"I know what you mean, Rachel," Sally said. "'Tis the way I feel about the Spaniard. I've never known why I'm so afraid of him. Whether 'tis his voice or his tone or his accent, every time I hear him speak, it makes me shudder."

"He was here last night with his pirate friends," Todd said. "The tavern was so busy, we had to help serve. I took the Spaniard his ale because Sally wouldn't." Todd shot Sally a superior glance.

But Rachel barely heard Todd. She was thinking too hard about what Sally had said. *Spaniard . . . his voice . . . makes me shudder . . .*

All at once the answer burst into Rachel's mind, and every part of her body seemed to burn with its scathing truth. It was Craven's *voice* that troubled her.

It was Craven's voice she had heard that moonless night on Skull Island . . . telling the Spaniard that he would kill him, make no mistake about it.

CHAPTER 12
NATE THE KNAVE

Breathlessly, Rachel told her friends what she was thinking.

"Rachel," Sally said with intensity. "Are you certain?"

Rachel nodded. Her throat was too dry to speak. She swallowed and then said slowly, "That night on the island, I couldn't stop thinking about what the big man had said. It bothered me terribly. And it kept on bothering me. For days and days afterward. I kept telling myself I should forget it, but I couldn't. Now I know why. It wasn't *what* he said so much as his voice. A part of me must have known his voice was familiar. And the last time I saw Craven, I felt even more uneasy, but I never put the two together until now."

"He's a pirate!" Todd declared. "I knew 'twas so. That eye of his—"

"Have a care, Todd," Sally said. "A missing eye don't make a man a pirate any more than does a missing leg.

You need proof to bring charges of such a crime, and we have none."

"We saw them go after their treasure," Todd insisted. "And pull it from the rocks in the lagoon."

"We don't know *what* they were going after," said Sally. "We never *saw* any treasure."

"They were digging on an island in the dark of night!" Todd cried.

"Digging on an island is *suspicious*," Sally said, "not illegal."

Rachel was a little calmer now and trying to think clearly. "That's the trouble. We can't prove that Craven has done anything more than act suspiciously."

"He was with the Spaniard," said Todd, "and *everybody* says *he's* a pirate."

"'Tis not proof, Todd!" Sally's voice rose impatiently.

Todd crossed his arms and poked out his lip. "'Tis to me."

"Wait," said Rachel. A plan was forming in her mind, though the very thought of it scared her to death. "Maybe there's a way we could discover what connection Craven really has to the Spaniard."

"How?" said Sally.

Rachel hesitated, taking a deep breath. "We could wait on the Spaniard's table one night when he and his friends come in the tavern, and try to listen to their conversation. Perhaps they'll mention Craven."

"Aye!" exclaimed Todd. "We shall serve them all the ale they can drink. *That* ought to loose their tongues."

Sally's eyes had gone big and round. "Eavesdrop on the *Spaniard*? What if he catches us?"

"I doubt he'll pay us any mind," Rachel said, as much to convince herself as Sally. "Especially if we keep the ale coming, as Todd suggested." She glanced at Todd, then back at Sally. "I can't see a better way of finding out Craven's game. Can you?"

After a long pause, Sally finally said, "Very well, I'll do it." Then she added fiercely, "Though I'll not be the one to hand the Spaniard his ale. He might see me trembling, and that would be the end of us."

"*I* shall serve him," Todd said with bravado. "He don't scare me a bit. Let's do it tonight."

"If we must do it," said Sally, "then tonight *would* be best. Mama will be out. She's going to visit a friend who's dangerous ill. Prudence will be glad for our help serving."

Sally gave Rachel a dress to wear when she came that evening. "Your clothes would do naught but attract attention," she said. "Which is the last thing we want."

Rachel ate her supper alone that night. Aunt Catherine wasn't feeling well, and Miranda, Mistress Brownlow told

Rachel, had sent word earlier that she would be dining with a friend. *Probably Mr. Craven,* Rachel thought with disgust.

After eating, Rachel told Mistress Brownlow she was tired and would retire early. Then she headed down the back stairway and out the courtyard gate. The warm light of candles and fireside shone from the houses Rachel passed, but the sight failed to comfort her as it usually did. She was far too nervous about the task ahead of her.

By the time Rachel reached the tavern, her stomach was churning. The taproom was even more crowded than usual, but Rachel easily picked out the men Todd called pirates. She recognized them. They were the brutish men Rachel had been afraid of when she came to the tavern on the night of Miranda's arrival. There were three of them, sitting at the same corner table, away from the other customers, but none of them looked like the Spaniard from the island. One of the men was small, with a red face and a large, bulbous nose. His companions were big men, one bald-headed with bushy eyebrows and the other with a long mustache and eyes black and round as a snake's.

Rachel spied Sally and Todd over by the bar, near the corner table. Prudence was scurrying from table to table and mopping her face with her apron. She seemed overwhelmed with handling so many customers. She glanced up as Rachel came in, gave her a quick smile and darted her eyes toward Sally and Todd, then returned her attention to serving.

Rachel had to walk by the corner table to get to Sally and Todd at the bar. Her heart thumped when she noticed the men's knives strapped to their belts. They were the only customers in the taproom who had them. Rachel thought of the long knives of the pirates who attacked the *Betsy Jo.* She shivered as she hurried past the men to the bar, where Sally was filling tankards at the tap and Todd was waiting with a tray.

"Where's the Spaniard?" Rachel said under her breath.

"He's not here," Todd said. "His friends came in without him tonight."

"Thanks be to heaven," Sally muttered, setting two tankards on Todd's tray.

Dismay leaped to Rachel's throat. "Now we'll never find out anything about Craven!"

Sally tried to console her. "Perhaps he'll come in later, Rachel. Besides, his friends will likely talk more free without him here. I know I would." Sally gave a little shudder.

"Aye," said Todd, "they're drinking more free, to be sure. We brought them three rounds already. Or is it four, Sally?"

"I don't know," Sally answered. "I've been too nervous to count. Mama will have our hides when she finds out how much ale we've given away." She filled another tankard and set it on the tray. "Though 'tis too late to worry about it now, I suppose. Take these on to their table, Todd. And let's be certain Mama's ale isn't wasted—listen carefully to every word they say and let us know if their conversation turns in the direction we want. Understand?"

"I shall get them talking," Todd said.

"Just listen." Sally's voice was firm. "We don't want to make them suspicious."

But Todd was already ambling to the pirates' table and setting their drinks down, chattering away. On the one hand, Rachel had to admire Todd's pluck. The pirates, with their savage-looking eyes and unshaven faces, made Rachel's skin crawl. They frightened her enough, even without the Spaniard. That, though, was what worried Rachel about Todd: he wasn't scared enough of the pirates. The way he was chattering to them, he was liable to say the wrong thing, and, with these men, saying the wrong thing could be dangerous. At the very least it could make them wary and unlikely to talk at all.

"Look at Todd," Rachel said to Sally. "He didn't hear a word you said. I'd best go over and take them another round, before Todd gets himself in trouble."

"Wait," Sally said. "I think Todd wants us both to come over. Look at him."

Rachel glanced over at Todd. He was beckoning wildly

to Sally and Rachel behind his back. A thrill tingled down Rachel's spine. Maybe the pirates were talking about Craven!

"You take them their drinks, Rachel," Sally said. She hastily filled more tankards. "I shall make some excuse in a minute for coming over—wipe the tables or something."

Rachel nodded. She set the drinks on a tray and took a moment to steady her hands and breathing; then she started forward. Once she reached earshot of the pirates, though, she stopped short. It wasn't Craven the pirates were talking about at all. It was an island, and it sounded like Skull Island!

"Went all over that bug-infested island," the pirate with the red face was saying, "looking for some cussed markers Cap'n Cordiaz said he left for us. Took half of last night to find the markers, and the other half to stash the goods under the rocks where he told us."

Rachel's heart was beating so loud she was afraid the pirates could hear it. It was all she could do to hold on to the tray and keep from dropping the drinks. She was afraid to move for fear the pirates would notice her and stop talking. She felt rather than saw Sally come over and start wiping the table beside the pirates'. Todd had fallen quiet, and the pirates seemed to have forgotten him.

In fact, the pirates continued as if all three children were invisible. "Ah, but Cap'n Cordiaz rewards you well, does he not?" A greedy light came into the bald pirate's eyes. "Surely you can share your profits with me. We'll outfit our own ship and be under way in a week."

"Hmph," said the snake-eyed pirate. "'Twill be a week at least till we get paid. Cordiaz won't pay us a shilling until old Nate looks the goods over and decides what he thinks they're worth."

"And Nate the Knave don't venture out on that island just any old time," said the red-faced pirate. "It has to be the new moon, y'see, the darkest night of the month. *He* won't take no chances, that one, that any living soul could connect him with us."

"You'll have to wait for your money, mate," said the snake-eyed pirate to the bald one, "the same as we wait for ours."

The bald pirate grumbled but agreed to wait, and their conversation turned to what they would do to amuse themselves in Charles Town for the next week. Rachel had been listening so intently, she had never served the pirates their drinks. Now she didn't think she could make herself do it, and she didn't think it would be a good idea anyway, since she was shaking all over. She caught Sally's eye, then Todd's, and as if by mutual agreement, the three of them headed to the back door of the tavern. They huddled outside and quickly whispered about what they had heard.

The children agreed the pirates must have been talking about *their* island—Skull Island. They didn't agree on what to make of the rest of the pirates' conversation.

Who was this Captain Cordiaz, and who was Nate the Knave? Todd was sure that Cordiaz was the Spaniard and Nate the Knave was Mr. Craven. But Sally and Rachel didn't think they should make any assumptions.

"'Tis a dangerous game we're playing," Sally said in a tight voice. "I for one must know for sure."

An image flashed into Rachel's mind: that night on the island, the man she believed was Craven, seizing his companion, beating him, threatening him. Then the way he looked up at the ridge, dead at the spot where she and Sally and Todd were crouching . . . Rachel's stomach knotted at the thought. "No," she said grimly. "We can't afford to make a mistake, not with a man like Craven."

Sally nodded. "It shouldn't be hard to learn the Spaniard's name. Mama may be able to tell us."

"That leaves the Knave," said Todd. "Shall I go to Craven's house and see if he answers to Nate?"

"Todd, I wish you'd take this seriously," scolded Sally. She turned to Rachel. "I don't suppose you ever heard your father use Craven's first name?"

Rachel shook her head. "Papa always called him 'Mr. Craven,' even when speaking directly to him." But an idea had come to her, though she wasn't sure she had the nerve to do it. It would involve betraying Papa's trust.

Cautiously Rachel spoke. "Craven would have to sign his full name on business correspondence, would he not?"

"I'd think so," said Sally, sounding puzzled. She waited for Rachel to explain.

"Papa keeps his business papers in his desk," Rachel said. "There's bound to be something official from Craven there—a letter or contract or something. I shall sneak down tonight and go through the drawers."

Todd's face flushed with excitement. "Then we'd have the rat in our trap."

"Perhaps," Rachel said. "Perhaps not. Nate the Knave—who knows whether that's a real name or a false one? 'Tis worth a try, though. *If* I can make myself go through with it."

Later that night, Rachel slipped out from under her coverlet. In her bare feet and gown, she crept to the bedroom door and opened it. The hall was dark and quiet. From the first floor below came the slow tick of the grandfather clock. Nothing else stirred in the house.

Rachel glided silently down the stairs and stood at the bottom, letting her eyes adjust to the moonlight that shone through the window over the front door. She glanced at the clock. Twelve midnight. At that moment the clock whirred and started striking. The first strike startled Rachel, but the second seemed to spur her to action. Quickly she padded to her father's office, pushed open the door, and entered. The clock was still striking. *Three . . . four . . . five . . .*

On the sixth gong, Rachel let the door thump shut behind her. The office was dark, with only a glimmer of moonlight showing around the edges of the curtain. Against the far wall, Rachel made out a black shape that she knew was Papa's desk. She would need more light for her task, yet she didn't dare light a candle. And if she opened the curtains, there was always the chance that passersby would see her, perhaps think the house was being robbed. Rachel fretted over what to do. The clock struck for a seventh time.

She would have to take the chance of being seen from outside. As the clock chimed eight and then nine and ten, Rachel pulled open the curtains. A ghostly light flooded the room. The clock struck eleven, twelve, then fell silent. The silence seemed to echo even louder than the gong of the clock . . . or was the echo only the sound of her pounding heart?

Rachel sat down in the hard wooden desk chair. Papa's desk was massive. Rachel saw that he had left the rolltop open and the lock unlocked. There was no need to lock it, thought Rachel guiltily, since Papa trusted that no one but he would use this room. She had such an attack of conscience then that she almost turned and fled, but she thought again of Craven, and she forced her hand to the large drawer at the bottom right. She would start there.

She shuffled through the papers within, straining in the dim light to scrutinize any documents bearing signatures. Then, upon a bill of sale for fifty barrels of rum, she found what she had been looking for. At the bottom of the page was a signature scrawled in large, bold letters: *Nathaniel F. Craven.*

"Nathaniel . . . Nate," Rachel whispered. "Craven *is* Nate the Knave."

CHAPTER 13
PIRATES' TREASURE

Back in bed, Rachel lay awake, trying to piece together what she thought was happening. Craven, it seemed, *was* doing business with pirates, just as she and Sally and Todd had suspected, and the Spaniard—Cordiaz—seemed to be Craven's associate, his go-between. Using the island as a delivery point, Craven bought stolen goods—like Rachel's necklace—from pirates, dirt cheap, then turned around and sold the goods to unsuspecting Charles Town merchants—like Papa—at market value. Those barrels of rum that Papa had bought from Craven were probably stolen, Rachel thought with outrage. Craven was lining his pockets with Papa's money!

Rachel thought of Craven's proposition to Miranda. Did he plan to involve her in cheating Charles Town merchants, perhaps even her own fiancé?

Would Miranda do such a thing? Rachel recalled the

fond glances she'd seen pass between Papa and Miranda. She thought of the admiration in Miranda's voice when she talked to Papa. Had it all been an act on Miranda's part to snag a rich husband?

Yet Rachel didn't doubt Papa's genuine affection for Miranda. Could he be so wrong about his future wife?

Then it occurred to Rachel that Miranda might believe her father really had become an honest business-man. Rachel wondered how Miranda truly felt about him. Could she possibly love her father as much as Rachel loved Papa?

Thinking of Papa made Rachel's heart ache, and a hopeless feeling rose inside her. What did it matter if she and Todd and Sally knew that Craven was buying pirates' plunder? They were only children, and who would listen to them when they couldn't provide a shred of solid evidence?

What they needed was proof that no one could deny. Where could they get proof?

The answer came to Rachel as clearly as the chime of the grandfather clock: *Skull Island.*

If she could only convince Todd and Sally to go back.

The next morning on her way to Madame Varnod's, Rachel stopped by the tavern to share her plan with Sally and Todd. After she told them, though, about discovering the bill of sale with Craven's signature, Rachel found she couldn't go on. It had just occurred to her what she would be asking of Sally and Todd: that they disobey their mother and perhaps put themselves in danger, all to help Rachel's father. It was a tremendous thing to ask of her friends, and Rachel didn't know if she had the right to do so.

Rachel's misgiving must have showed in her face, because Sally furrowed her brow and said, "What's wrong, Rachel? Is there something you've not told us?"

Rachel hesitated. Fleetingly she considered going to the island alone, but she knew that would be pointless. Her plan depended on moving those rocks in the lagoon, and she couldn't lift them without Sally and Todd's help. She swallowed and plunged on. "Everything we've learned about Craven is useless, Sally, unless we have some evidence against him that we can take to the sheriff. And the only way I can think of to get the evidence we need"— Rachel took a deep breath—"is to go back to Skull Island."

"And pick up the pirate's treasure before Craven gets to it!" Todd interrupted.

Rachel nodded slowly. "If the treasure is something small, we'll bring it back and show it to the sheriff."

"Spanish gold!" Todd blurted out.

Only half hearing him, Rachel swept on. "If what we find is too big to carry on the skiff, we'll hide it on the island and tell the sheriff where it is. He and his men can go back and get it later. With that kind of evidence, the sheriff should have no qualms about going out to the island on the first night of the new moon to catch Craven when he comes to pick up his goods."

Sally, wide-eyed and open-mouthed, was shaking her head. "I can't believe, Rachel, you would even *think* of going back to that island."

"I don't *want* to do it, any more than you do," Rachel said. "But I do want to see Craven's business exposed and him convicted before Papa comes under suspicion."

"'Twouldn't surprise me none," said Todd, "if there's a reward for returning pirate's plunder."

Sally ignored Todd. "What if we run into the pirates on the island? What if that awful Spaniard is there?" she asked. "Or even Craven himself?"

Rachel had already considered these possibilities. "I don't think we need concern ourselves with the pirates. They've dropped the goods on the island, so their part of the bargain's finished. And it sounds to me as if Craven and the Spaniard go to the island together and only in the dark of a new moon."

"There was a quarter moon last night," Todd said, "so you see, Sally, we're safe."

Sally frowned. "I don't *feel* safe." She looked away, and for a moment Rachel was afraid she was going to refuse. When she turned back, her face was pale but there was a determined set to her mouth. "You didn't give up on being my friend, Rachel, when it was hard for you, and I shan't give up on being yours. I'll go with you to the island one more time, but, pray, don't ever, *ever* ask me to do it again."

Rachel knew what it cost Sally to agree. She threw her arms around her friend. "I shall be in your debt as long as I live, Sally Pugh." Then, resting her hands on Sally's shoulders, Rachel asked earnestly, "Can you go today?"

"The sooner 'tis over with, the better," Sally said. "We might as well go this afternoon at low tide."

"I'll come straight here from Madame Varnod's," said Rachel. "I'll meet you in the stable at two o'clock."

When Rachel stepped out of Madame Varnod's front door that afternoon, she was astonished to find that the temperature had dropped sharply since morning. The sun was shining, but the air felt clammy and smelled of salt mud, which meant the wind was blowing from the east, across the creeks and marshes of the Ashley. Rachel shivered, both from the chill and from the knowledge that the wind would make the coming task all the harder, for they would be rowing against it out to Skull Island.

Todd and Sally were waiting for Rachel in the stable, and before long, the three were making their slow way across the sound. By the time they reached the island, the sun shone dimly through gray clouds, and fingers of fog lay across the marsh.

"We'd best hurry," Sally said, quickening her strokes on the oars. "By nightfall this fog could swallow the entire island." A pause. "That is . . . if you still want to carry this out, Rachel."

Rachel was no more eager than Sally to grope through those dark woods in a cloak of fog. "How long do you think we have before the fog starts moving across the island?" she asked.

"Truthfully," Sally said, "there's no way to tell. Could be a good while, for the fog hasn't yet begun to move up the creek. Could be that it will not move at all . . ." Her voice trailed off uncertainly.

"We've plenty of time," Todd said with bluster. "I wish you girls wouldn't talk so much."

"'Tis up to Rachel," Sally said, looking toward Rachel, waiting.

Rachel made her decision. "Let's go on," she said, "but let's do it quickly."

They pulled the skiff up onto the creek bank and hid it under some brush—just in case. Then they headed into the woods. As they went further into the forest, Rachel noticed patches of mist hanging in swampy areas between the trees. Anxiety tugged at her ever so slightly. Had her decision to go on been a foolish one?

Rachel glanced back at Sally, a few strides behind her. Sally's mouth was drawn into a tight line, but if she felt they ought to turn back, she didn't say so. Rachel trudged on. They came to the fork in the creek and then to the deer trail. They followed the trail up the hill, until they heard the roar of the breakers. "Almost there now," Rachel said to Todd and picked up her pace. When they reached the boulder and Rachel spied the carved symbol, she felt suddenly breathless. Was it from the climb, she wondered, or from her own nervous excitement?

Before long, Rachel was sure, she would have in her hands the pirates' treasure—her means of helping Papa. Spurred by the thought, she rushed ahead of Sally and Todd to the top of the ridge. When she gazed down the other side, though, her heart flip-flopped. A low blanket of fog covered the lagoon and was creeping over the dunes from the sea, like a great, writhing snake.

Soon, just as Sally had predicted, the island was likely to be swallowed whole.

Rachel's mind flitted uneasily between options. Should they give up on the treasure and head back across the island, while they could still safely find their way? Or should they take a chance that they could beat the fog?

Sally and Todd had now come up beside her. Todd was squinting and looking down into the fog. "I don't see the pile of stones where the treasure's hid," he said.

Rachel strained into the mist. She could barely make out the lagoon itself. She thought she saw a dark mass in the middle that would have to be the stones, yet she couldn't be sure. Perhaps she was only seeing what she wanted to see. Were the stones still there? What if they weren't? What if Craven *had* seen her and Sally and Todd on the ridge that night and had gotten suspicious and moved the ballast stones somewhere else?

The stones *had* to be there, Rachel thought desperately. And she had to go find them. But how could she ask Sally and Todd to go into the fog?

Just then Sally stepped up behind her. "'Tis like a thing alive, that fog, and coming in fast," she said. She tugged at Rachel's arm. "We should get on with our task, Rachel, and get off the island while we can still see."

Rachel couldn't quite believe she had heard Sally right. "You mean . . . you're willing to go on?"

"'Course I am," said Sally. Now she was so close that Rachel could see beads of perspiration on Sally's forehead. Sally was scared stiff, Rachel realized, yet her voice was steady. "I gave my pledge as a friend to help you, and I'll not betray my word because of a fog. We know the island well enough. As long as we have daylight, we can find our way to the cove, I think."

Dear, brave Sally! Where could Rachel have found a truer friend? Not among her "high-class" schoolmates, Rachel was certain. Her throat swelled with gratitude and affection. "Thank you," Rachel choked out. She hoped Sally understood she was speaking of their friendship more than anything.

Sally gave a grim little smile and squeezed her hand.

Then, without speaking, Sally started down the hill. Rachel followed, and Todd came behind. Soon they were engulfed by the mist.

Once the children were *in* the fog, though, instead of looking down at it, it didn't seem so daunting. It was like walking through smoke, Rachel thought. She could see ten yards ahead, maybe twenty. Farther than that, there was nothing but whiteness. Rachel walked on with Sally and Todd, knowing the lagoon was there but not seeing it. Then, suddenly, the lagoon seemed to appear out of nowhere, its water silvery in the mist. Rachel stopped to take off her shoes and set them on the shore, then stepped into the frigid water, along with Sally and Todd. The water lapped insistently against their ankles and pushed toward the shore. "Tide's coming in," Sally commented. "We got here none too soon."

Rachel's toes tingled as the three waded out toward the middle of the lagoon. Then, almost as if it had jumped out of the mist, the pile of ballast stones materialized, rising like a dark mountain from the water. It was still there!

The pyramid was higher than it appeared from a distance—about double Todd's height—and built of stones of all sizes, many of them much larger stones than Rachel had hoped. For a moment the children just stood and stared up at that great mountain. "I'm not sure we can move those big stones at the top," Sally said miserably.

Rachel became aware of the push of the incoming tide on her legs, of her skirt growing wetter and wetter. Here they stood staring, while the tide was slowly reclaiming the ballast stones. There was no time to waste. "We'll have to try," Rachel said.

Climbing on all fours, the children scaled the pile of rocks. It took all three of them, sweating and straining, to shove the top ballast stone and send it rolling down the side. Stone by stone, then, the children uncapped the pyramid, until they could finally peer inside. There, half covered by water, was a small wooden barrel.

This one barrel was "the goods" the pirates had left for Craven? Rachel was disappointed. She had expected more than this. How much could a single barrel be worth?

"'Tis not much of a treasure," Todd said, echoing Rachel's thoughts. "I can't believe pirates would bother with one puny barrel of anything."

Sally shrugged. "We're not after treasure, Todd. We only need evidence to convict Mr. Craven."

"Sally's right," Rachel said, as much to herself as to Todd. "Let's open the barrel and see what's inside."

"How?" Todd asked. "We've nothing to use to pry off the lid."

Rachel thought. "We'll drop a rock on it, bash it in. I just hope the barrel's not full of rum."

The children chose a stone that seemed not too large to lift over the top of the barrel but large enough to break the barrel open. They stood on the pyramid and, with all the strength they could muster, heaved the rock onto the barrel. With a loud crack, the lid splintered, and Rachel felt her jaw drop in disbelief.

The barrel was full of brick-sized silver ingots.

"'*Tis* a treasure!" Todd cried. "A real pirate's treasure!"

Sally nodded, her eyes shining. "There's a fortune in that barrel, I'd wager." She turned to Rachel. "What do you think Craven planned to do with it?"

"Buy some ships, perhaps," Rachel said bitterly, "to cheat some other town's merchants." She crouched and picked up one of the silver bricks, felt its cold, hard smoothness. "It doesn't matter, though, does it, for Craven won't gain a shilling of *this* pirate's treasure. Instead, 'twill be his downfall, when we show these ingots to the sheriff." Rachel felt a sense of triumph.

But she was also gripped by the need to hurry. The lagoon's water was licking at the sides of the barrel, rising as they watched. Rachel spoke swiftly. "Let's take with us as many of the ingots as we can. We shall have to leave the rest, for there's no time to bother with hiding them."

The friends gathered three or four bars each and slogged back through the lagoon. Upon reaching the shore, they were all soaked to the bone and shivering from a stiff ocean wind that set the fog swirling about them. Rachel put on her shoes, and they struggled back up the ridge, the heavy ingots slowing their progress. Rachel looked back from the top of the ridge at the blanket of fog below. It was growing, slinking up the ridge after them like a stalking cat. A cold chill ran down Rachel's spine. She promised herself she wouldn't look back again.

The woods were murky with mist, a mist that thickened even as the children walked. By the time they reached the creek, Rachel could see no more than a few yards in front of her. Without speaking, the children followed the creek on and on, past the branch that curved off to the myrtle grove and sinkhole—at least what Rachel *thought* was that branch, for she'd lost all sense of direction in the fog. Rachel's arms ached from carrying the heavy ingots. The creek seemed endless. Rachel felt sure they ought to have reached the cove by now. Had they taken a wrong turn somewhere?

Just as Rachel opened her mouth to ask that question of Sally, she clamped it shut tight. She'd heard something, something that sounded like the tramp of feet, somewhere in the mist up ahead. By the look of alarm on her friends' faces, Rachel knew Sally and Todd had heard it, too. Rachel's thoughts were suddenly frenzied: What to do? Where to go? Hide or run?

But there was no chance to think through or to act, for breaking out of the fog ahead was a figure made ghostly by the mist and waning light: the figure of Mr. Craven.

CHAPTER 14
HUNTED

Time came to a stop as Craven stared at Rachel, his good eye hard upon the ingots in her arms. Rachel could not look away. Her mind worked dully. Craven came only at night, the pirates had said. Why was he here now, in daylight?

'Tis the fog. He thought 'twas safe in the fog.

The answer came to Rachel as clearly as if it had been spoken aloud, and it seemed to release her from paralysis. *If the fog could cover Craven, maybe it could cover them, too.*

Rachel yanked backward on Sally and Todd. "Run," she murmured. "Hide in the myrtle grove." The children turned and fled back the way they had come, up the creek. Craven shouted something—Rachel thought it was her name—but the sound, like Craven, fell away and vanished in the mist.

Then, behind them, somewhere in the fog, came a crashing and a pounding of feet. Craven was coming after them.

Fear beating in her throat, Rachel ran faster. Todd and Sally ran faster, too. They scrambled through brush and leaped over logs, running, running through the veil of mist. They ran until Rachel thought her arms would drop off from carrying the ingots, until every breath burned her lungs. Where, oh, where was the branch of the creek?

Finally, they stopped to get their bearings, and they didn't hear Craven behind them. "We've . . . lost him." Todd could hardly speak for panting so hard. He collapsed onto the forest floor. "'Tis a good thing. I don't think I can carry these ingots another step."

"Do you think he's given up?" Sally leaned against a pine tree, trying to catch her breath.

Rachel listened. A few crickets had begun to sing, but in that great shroud of whiteness, nothing else stirred. Yet Rachel could not shake the certainty that Craven was out there somewhere. "He's too big to move as quickly as we," she said. "But I don't think he would give up so easily. He's behind us somewhere. We must keep going."

The children allowed themselves a few more minutes' rest—as long as they dared—then went on at a brisk walk, for Todd declared he was too tired to go faster. The bank of the creek was becoming less steep. Rachel felt sure they were near the branch, but the crickets were singing in earnest now. There couldn't be more than an hour of daylight left. They had to reach the myrtle grove soon or give up the idea entirely, Rachel realized with a sick feeling. After dark the sinkhole would be as much a threat as Craven.

Wind rustled the leaves of the trees, and Rachel caught a whiff of bayberries—a blessed smell—and then, there was the branch. Now it was only a short distance to the myrtle grove. The children moved cautiously through the clumps of shrubs, alert for the warning whir of a rattler ready to strike. Just as they cleared the bayberry bushes, they did hear something, but it wasn't a rattlesnake. It was something much more menacing— the low drone of voices from out in the mist, and *it sounded as if the voices were almost upon them.*

Rachel would never know what caused Todd to panic, but the next thing she knew, he screamed in terror, dropped his ingots, and bolted into the fog.

"Todd!" Sally cried. She flung down her ingots and took off after him. In an instant she disappeared into the fog.

It was madness, *madness,* to dash off the trail into the fog! Rachel wanted to shout it out, call for her friends to come back, but she heard the voices again—louder, nearer—excited voices, and footsteps hurrying toward her. Craven and the Spaniard, she thought, both of them after us!

Rachel was seized by a panic so strong it seemed to strangle her. The silver bricks fell from her arms, and, like a deer struck by an arrow, she too fled into the mist, running blindly. Terror drove her on and on, until she finally collapsed, so spent she could scarcely move. She lay gasping for breath, staring into the trees and the mist, straining to listen: for Craven, for Sally and Todd. She heard nothing but the sounds of the forest—the crickets, the tree frogs, the distant *cuckoo* of a bird.

What had happened to Sally and Todd? They seemed to have vanished into thin air. She was alone and lost in the forest, with night coming on and Craven hunting her down. It was also getting colder; a steady wind was blowing. Rachel struggled against despair. She had to think clearly, decide what to do. She raised herself up to a sitting position and rubbed her shoulders to warm herself.

Rachel noticed that she could see a little more clearly than she could only a moment ago. Yes, she was in a stand of pine trees, and there was a clump of shrubs with red blossoms, and there a palmetto bush, its spiny leaves rattling in the breeze. The wind was thinning out the fog!

At first Rachel was relieved. Perhaps she could figure out where she was and find her way to the myrtle grove. Perhaps Todd and Sally would even be waiting for her there. But then a frightening thought struck Rachel. If *she* could see more clearly, *Craven* could see more clearly, too. It would be much easier now for Craven to track her down.

She would just have to be more careful, Rachel decided. She stood up and gazed around her. This stand of pines looked familiar, very familiar. Rachel's senses stirred with excitement. She recognized it now! This was the copse of trees where she and Sally had seen the snowy egret, where they had found the first of the symbols carved on one of the pines—which meant that she wasn't far from the myrtle grove.

Tentatively Rachel moved among the pines and the moss-hung oaks, trying to recall from which direction she and Sally had come that day. She thought she remembered this carpet of running evergreen, those large ferns. Trouble was, it all looked so different, with dusk deepening and the tentacles of mist twisting about the trees, now obscuring, now revealing.

Then a gust of wind caught the mist and swept it up in an eddy, and Rachel's heart nearly stopped. There, off in the forest, she had caught a glimpse of Craven!

Had he seen her?

For a terrified moment, Rachel wrestled with her thoughts. If Craven *hadn't* seen her, her only hope lay in staying still, for if she ran, he would hear her and come after her. But if he *had* seen her and she didn't move, he would catch her. Rachel felt the blood pounding in her head as she wavered in indecision.

Then, through the mist that was slowly drifting back to earth, Craven spoke. "Miss Howell. Is that you? I've been looking for you." His voice was gentle, full of concern, nothing like the angry growl Rachel had heard that night from the ridge.

Doubt flickered through her mind. Had she been too eager to jump to conclusions about Craven? Could she have been wrong about seeing him in the lagoon?

No, Rachel told herself firmly. *I know it was Craven. He* is *a knave. And a swindler and a fraud. He's trying to trick me.*

Rachel started walking, on silent cat's feet, past the running evergreen and the fern, walking, following her instinct, toward the myrtle grove. Dusk was falling fast. The trunks of the oaks were dense with darkness, and their mossy hair stirred eerily above Rachel's head. Rachel tried to shake off her growing apprehension. Where was Craven? Was he following her?

The ground became springy under Rachel's feet. She knew she was near the myrtle grove . . . and near the sinkhole. She must be very careful, measure every step. Here the fog was heavier. It seemed to gather around Rachel like a shroud. She could hardly see at all through the web of white. Then waxy myrtle leaves brushed her face, and relief poured over her. She had made it to the grove!

Were Todd and Sally hiding here somewhere? Rachel didn't dare call out and risk Craven hearing. She resolved to find her friends somehow, wherever they were. But now she must keep Craven from finding *her.*

She dropped to all fours and crawled into the tangled shrubs, far enough to be well hidden, but not too far: the sinkhole was just on the other side of the bushes. Scarcely daring to breathe, she waited.

Then Rachel heard Craven again, somewhere close but beyond her field of vision. "Why are you running from your father's best friend?"

Her father's best friend. Could that be true?

Mr. Craven is one of the most respected men in Charles Town. Papa's voice echoed in Rachel's mind. Suddenly she was flooded with uncertainty. How could Papa have been so wrong about Craven? Again she wondered if it was she who was wrong.

"Miss Howell."

Craven was nearer. It sounded as if he was coming up behind her. Rachel scrunched herself around and peered out toward his voice, but she could only see a little way, into leaves and the muddy sinkhole . . . and fog.

"The wind is rising," Craven said, still nearer. "There's a storm blowing in. We need to get off the island."

The wind *was* rising. Rachel could hear it whistling far above her through the pines. She didn't know what frightened her more—Craven . . . or the prospect of a storm. Storms in Charles Town, she had heard, could be deadly. Which would be worse: to face Craven, or to be caught in a storm—alone—on Skull Island?

"Miss Howell, I know you're here somewhere."

Now Rachel could see Craven's legs, a few yards away, on the other side of the sinkhole. He was coming toward her, his heavy black boots sinking slightly with every step. Rachel swallowed repeatedly, fear thickening inside her.

Her thoughts came in rapid succession: *He doesn't know about the sinkhole . . . I can dash out . . . run for the cove . . . if he chases me, he'll be caught in the mud . . . he'll never get out . . . but how could I do that . . . leave him here to die . . . might be my only chance to escape . . .*

Suddenly Rachel's thoughts stopped dead. Had she really heard what she thought she heard?

"Rachel! Are you here? Rachel!"

She had! It was Sally, out there in the fog, calling her. Rachel's heart lifted at the familiar sound of Sally's voice, then, just as quickly, it froze. Now Craven would go after Sally!

Rachel didn't hesitate a moment. "Sally!" she yelled. "Run for your life! Craven's here!"

Then everything happened with lightning speed. Craven barreled forward and howled as he dropped into the sinkhole. Rachel scrambled out of the myrtle grove and ran the other way. The wind whipped her hair and dress. It moaned through the trees and whisked the fog about her. Running feet, too heavy to be Sally's, pounded toward Rachel. Then came a light, bobbing rapidly, and husky voices.

"I think she's here!" someone shouted.

There was no time for Rachel to react. Out of the fog burst two men, one carrying a lantern, the other a pistol. The lantern's light licked through the fog, and Rachel saw the men's faces. The one with the pistol she recognized as the sheriff, and the one with the lantern was . . . Papa.

Somehow Papa must have found out about Craven and followed him to the island! Rachel tried to cry out, but her throat was too tight. Instead, she heard Papa's voice exclaim, "Rachel! Thank God you're safe!" and saw him striding toward her.

Rachel fell into his arms, sobbing.

CHAPTER 15
HOME FIRES BURNING

The hours afterward would never be clear in Rachel's mind. Though she knew what was happening, it all seemed a dream or a part of the fog: Papa embracing her and trying to talk to her over the sound of the wind, Sally and Todd appearing with one of the sheriff's men, Papa and the sheriff pulling Craven from the mud and putting him under arrest, the hurry to get back to the boats and across the sound before the storm hit, the squall starting just as they came in sight of Charles Town.

The storm was raging in earnest by the time Rachel and Papa delivered Todd and Sally to the tavern, the rain coming down in sheets and the wind whipping it mercilessly into their faces. Mistress Pugh entreated Papa and Rachel to stay until the rain let up, but Papa said they had best ease the minds of those waiting for them at home. He thanked her, and he and Rachel went back out into the storm.

Even wrapped in Papa's big cloak, Rachel was soaked to the bone and so cold she was numb. She had to bow her head as she walked to keep the rain from stinging her face. She couldn't even think about the questions spinning through her mind, much less ask them. It took all her effort just to struggle home.

And then when they finally arrived, when Papa shut their own front door behind them, the warmth of the house was almost too much for Rachel. Her head swam, and she suddenly felt so weary she could hardly stand. Her knees started to buckle, but Papa was there, steadying her, looking anxiously down at her. She saw the streaks of mud on his face, the deep lines in his forehead, the stubble on his chin, flecked with gray. Papa looked weary, too—and old.

On Rachel's tongue were words she wanted to say, but she didn't have a chance. Miranda and Aunt Catherine were rushing to them from the parlor, Aunt Catherine saying how worried they'd been and how glad they were to see Rachel safe, and Miranda exclaiming over Rachel but so flustered that Rachel could make little sense of what she was saying. It was Aunt Catherine who seemed to have her head; she was the one who noticed the pool of water on the floor where Rachel and Papa were dripping, and who insisted they immediately get changed and come back down to warm by the fire. Only then did Miranda seem to come to her senses, to see Rachel's and Papa's bedraggled state. "Oh, yes," she said. "You must get out of those filthy clothes. Where on earth did you *get* that dress, Rachel?"

That dress. It was the same disdainful tone Miranda had had for Sally and Todd, and it incensed Rachel. Her jaws ached with holding back the angry words she wanted to say. So she said nothing, nothing at all, just whirled and fled to her room.

Rachel purposely took a long time changing in order to let her temper cool. Her resentment was still smoldering, though, when she came back down, and it didn't help at all to see from the foyer that Papa and Miranda were sitting together on the settee in the parlor. They were talking about Rachel—they and Aunt Catherine. Rachel heard them as she approached. "I blame myself for her running away," Miranda was saying. "I shudder to think what might have happened to her out on that island in the fog, with . . . with . . ." For some reason, Miranda didn't finish her sentence.

"Thank God," Aunt Catherine said, "you came home when you did and went after her, John."

Rachel stopped in her tracks. *Papa had* not *come to the island looking for Craven, he had come looking for* her. Papa had gone out in that ghastly fog looking for *her.* Rachel's heart swelled. She wanted to rush to Papa and throw her arms around him. But how could she, with Miranda there beside him? Why must Miranda always intrude?

At that moment Papa noticed Rachel in the doorway and beckoned to her. "Come, come, Rachel," he said. "We've been waiting for you."

Rachel walked slowly into the parlor. A fire crackled in the grate, and the settee and chairs had been drawn up before it. Aunt Catherine sat in her favorite upholstered chair on Papa's left. The maple tea table next to the settee had been spread with the tea service and a plate of Mistress Brownlow's macaroons.

"Sit here, Rachel," Miranda said, patting the damask chair beside her. "Mistress Brownlow has made your favorite macaroons, and I wouldn't let your father touch them until you got here. Have one, lamb." She held out a cookie to Rachel.

Rachel sat down heavily in the chair. Who did Miranda think she was, using Papa's pet name for Rachel? Miranda was acting as if she were already married to Papa, as if she were already Rachel's stepmother, and they were all one happy little family. Yet Miranda had shown in Papa's absence where her loyalty lay—not with Papa and Rachel, but with her real family: her father, Mr. Craven.

"Thank you. I'm not hungry," Rachel said, pulling away from Miranda's hand. Miranda drew back, a hurt look on her face.

"Rachel?" Papa set his teacup down with a *clink* on the saucer. "What's wrong with you?" He was frowning.

Everything Rachel wanted to tell Papa about the last

few days flew to her mind, but how could she start?
How could she begin to tell him how he'd been betrayed
by Miranda and by Craven?

Rachel nervously fingered the ruffled sleeve of her
shift. "Papa, there's . . . something that you should
know." She stopped for a moment, unnerved by Papa's
disapproving expression; then, shooting a guilty glance
at Miranda, she pressed on. "Miranda—she's . . . well . . .
she's Mr. Craven's daughter."

There. She had said it. Rachel flopped her hands into
her apron. After keeping her secret from Papa so long, she
felt a sense of relief. She waited for Papa's reaction. Would
he be shocked? Angry? Would he even believe her?

None of those responses would have surprised Rachel,
but Papa's reply did. "Yes, she is," Papa said calmly. "How
did you find out?"

Rachel felt herself flush. "You mean you already knew?"

"Only since this afternoon," Papa said, "when I came
home and found the whole household in an uproar because
you were missing."

"We'd had the servants out looking for you everywhere,
dear," Aunt Catherine said. "And then Miranda remembered your friends at the tavern and sent a servant there.
The children's mother said they were missing as well, and
since you and Miranda had had an argument, we assumed
you children had all run away together. Mistress Pugh
thought you might have gone to an island where the three

of you had . . . uh . . . apparently been going regularly."
Aunt Catherine looked as if she were embarrassed at
having to mention Rachel's wrongdoing.

Rachel's cheeks burned. Papa already knew, then,
about her disobedience. She was afraid to look at him,
but she made herself. His gaze was steady but not angry.
"I'm sorry I disobeyed you, Papa," Rachel said. "If you
only knew why I did it . . ."

"Tell us," Papa said gently. He leaned forward slightly
as if to encourage her.

So Rachel told them, told them everything, tentatively at first—it was hard to speak honestly in front of
Miranda—but, in the rush of her words, Rachel soon
forgot everyone but Papa. She told him about her friendship with Todd and Sally, their adventures on Skull Island,
and the way they uncovered Mr. Craven's dirty dealings
with pirates.

Then came the hard part: telling Papa about Craven
and Miranda's relationship. Miranda was silent as Rachel
related the incident with the pearls and explained how
she followed Miranda to Craven's house, then how she
read the letter Craven had sent to Miranda and figured
out that Craven had involved Miranda in his illicit
business.

"I'm sorry to be the one to tell you," Rachel said,
staring down at the buckles on her shoes. She couldn't
bear to look at Papa. She felt Miranda's eyes upon her,

but Rachel refused to look up. Miranda probably hated her now, and Rachel didn't care.

But when Miranda responded, her voice was filled with grief, not anger. "Rachel, you really think me capable of betraying your father?"

Rachel was shocked at the words that jumped from her lips. "You lied to him, didn't you?"

"Rachel!" Papa said, his eyes flashing. "You will not speak to Miranda that way."

"No, John, I deserve it," Miranda said quietly. "And Rachel deserves an explanation for my behavior." In a rustle of skirts she rose and went to the hearth, where she poked absently at the fire. "Let me tell you about my father, Rachel." She pronounced the word *father* with bitterness.

She spoke rapidly, as if in a hurry to be done. "Once upon a time, his name was Victor LeBoyer. He was a respectable planter in Barbados, where I was born. But when I was eight years old, he abruptly decided to become a merchantman. He bought a ship, outfitted it, and told my mother he was sailing to England for merchandise. We found out later he hadn't become a merchantman at all"—she jabbed at a log with the poker—"he'd become a pirate." A violent jab.

Embers rained from the log, the fire flared, and Rachel sucked in her breath. A pirate! She had never dreamed Craven had been *that* much of a scoundrel.

Somewhere in the house a servant slammed a door, and Miranda continued. "The scandal for my mother was unbearable, as you might imagine, so while Father was away, we fled Barbados and came to New York, then to Philadelphia. For years my mother worried that Father would find us and strike back at her for leaving him, but either he never tried to find us or he never could, for we did not hear from him again."

"Then he showed up in Charles Town," Rachel said, understanding.

"Yes, then he showed up in Charles Town." Miranda returned the poker to its stand and brushed her hands together, as if to rid them of something soiling them. "Actually, Father had been living here for years under an assumed name, pretending to be an honest merchant."

"He had me fooled," Papa said roughly, "and all of Charles Town."

"Oh, Father was always that way." There was a grimace on Miranda's face. "So smooth-talking he could charm the fangs off a snake. And I knew that about him, yet I let him charm me into believing he had changed. But that came later. On that first meeting, I was simply too shocked at seeing him here to know how to react, so I pretended to you, John, that I didn't know him. After that it became more and more difficult to tell you . . . and easier and easier to fall under Father's spell. I had no idea I was playing right into his hands."

What did Miranda mean, playing into her father's hands? But Rachel had no chance to ask, for Miranda swept on. "It felt so wonderful to have a father again—Rachel, surely you understand that. I wanted to think that Mother had been wrong about him, that he was really a good person and that he loved me."

Miranda fell silent. The fire snapped and crackled, and something roused inside of Rachel, something long buried and forgotten. Was it that feeling of warmth toward Miranda that Rachel had felt once, ever so briefly? Rachel closed her eyes. She didn't want to acknowledge it. She opened them again when Miranda continued.

Miranda seemed to be choosing her words with care, yet she spoke as if they were directed to no one but herself. "I thought the pearls proved Father's love. He said they were very rare and that he'd had the necklace made especially for me. Then, when Rachel said the necklace was hers, that it had been stolen from her by pirates, I was devastated. It would have been proof that Father was lying, that he *hadn't* changed, that he was still at heart a pirate. I didn't want to accept it. Which is why I spoke so viciously to you, Rachel. I'm deeply sorry."

Rachel could no longer deny the sympathy stirring inside her. She remembered how it felt to so desperately want a father. "That's why you were crying," Rachel said softly.

Miranda nodded. "Inwardly, though, I suspected the

truth, and I went to Father's house, angry, ready to confront him. But slippery old eel that he is, he fed me a story of his innocence, so earnest, so convincing, I swallowed it whole."

A deep line appeared between Miranda's brows. "Father claimed he'd been deceived by the jeweler, and he would have the man arrested for fraud. He assured me many times over of his love and professed how much he regretted all the years of my life he had missed. I wanted desperately to believe him, and I think I went home that night doing so.

"Yet I spent a restless night. I felt terrible about our argument, Rachel"—Miranda paused to look at her—"and I resolved to apologize and return the necklace to you. The next morning, though, I overslept, and when I came down for breakfast, Aunt Catherine told me you had already left for school. It was then that my world began to crumble." Miranda sank to the settee and buried her face in her hands. Papa laid a hand on Miranda's back.

Rachel felt a pang of jealousy that she tried to ignore. "I don't understand," she said.

"That's when the letters from your father arrived." Aunt Catherine set her teacup on the table. "One for you and one for Miranda."

"What did Miranda's letter say?" The question escaped Rachel's lips before she even thought about its inappropriateness.

Papa answered. "I released Miranda from our engagement, explaining that I now had no means to provide for her. I thought I was doing the honorable thing . . ." His voice trailed off. He looked pained.

Rachel remembered her own anguish when she read Papa's letter. Again she felt a grudging sympathy for Miranda.

When Miranda dropped her hands, Rachel saw that her face was streaked with tears. "I know you meant well, John." Miranda wiped her face with her sleeve.

"Oh, dear," said Aunt Catherine, "have a handkerchief, please." She pulled a handkerchief from her apron and passed it to Miranda.

Miranda took the handkerchief and dabbed at her eyes. "I'm sorry to weep so, John, but you can't imagine how your letter distressed me. I took to my room, too upset to think. There I remained for hours, trying to sort out my emotions."

"I want you to know, John," Aunt Catherine broke in, "that Miranda didn't tell me what was in your letter. I had no idea how upset she was. I thought she was in her room reading. So when another letter was brought by messenger, I sent it up with a servant instead of going myself." She turned to Miranda. "I feel as if I failed you, dear, when you needed me."

Miranda seemed to have regained her composure. "You couldn't have known that the letter was from Father.

And you surely couldn't have known how he was trying to use me."

"Trying to use you?" Rachel said. "For his pirate business?"

"I wish that it had been so simple." Miranda sighed deeply, as if she were alone in the room. "You remember that Father's note mentioned an argument we had had the previous evening?"

Rachel nodded, yet her conscience twitched. She knew she'd had no right to read that letter. Rachel had the uncomfortable thought that perhaps she'd been harder on Miranda than she was on herself.

Miranda's eyes fixed on the fire, then went dull. Her voice, though, was thick with emotion. "The argument concerned my marriage to your father, Rachel. John Howell wasn't worthy of me, Father railed, now that he'd lost all his money. Father wanted me to return with him to the Indies, where he would choose a proper husband for me. I told Father I wouldn't consider it, that I cared deeply for John and intended to marry him, rich or poor."

Rachel didn't miss the warm look Papa gave Miranda.

"Father let it drop, and I thought the matter was closed. I never dreamed to what lengths Father would go, and had gone already, to get his way."

"But you *gave* him his way," Rachel blurted out. "You rushed to accept his proposal—"

"No!" Miranda's hands went to the edge of the settee, where she gripped it tightly. "His note infuriated me. He was so sure of his hold over me. He just knew I would change my mind, do what he wanted. It made me so angry I ripped up the hat he had given me. And I did rush out—yes—but to turn him down." She was shaking all over.

"It was then Father showed me his true colors. He turned absolutely livid, bellowed at me, with his eyes blazing. He called me an ungrateful daughter, and worse things, which I won't repeat. He said I would never see him again, nor a penny of his money. And he told me . . . he told me what he had done to John . . ." Miranda broke down, her chest heaving with silent sobs. Papa put his arm around her.

"What did he do to you, Papa?" Rachel said. But looking at Papa's tight face, she knew. "It was Mr. Craven who ruined you, wasn't it?"

Papa's eyes hardened. He jerked his head in assent.

"But why? Why would he ruin his own business partner?"

"Craven hadn't been my partner long, you may recall," Papa said. "In fact, he approached me at Saint Philip's on the very day my engagement to Miranda was announced. He congratulated me, then made the business offer. I was flattered, and I never put the two together."

Miranda's chin came up. "Father hatched his plan

for revenge sitting there in church; I know he did—the old hypocrite." Her words had a fierce bite.

"Revenge?" Now Rachel was confused.

"I was just part of his plan," Papa said, "to get back at Miranda's mother."

Miranda, tight-lipped, explained. "Father thought my mother had done him a great wrong by leaving him, and it had festered inside him all these years. He would have done anything, sacrificed anything, for revenge. He said so himself, in those very words, when we argued. He wanted to hurt my mother to the core, and what better way than to win me back and carry me away with him to Barbados—in essence, disappear with me, just as Mother had done to him.

"Of course, his whole plan hinged on my not marrying John"—Miranda glanced at Papa—"and how could I marry a man who was penniless? Well, Father had no trouble fixing that. Robbing people comes naturally to him. I have no doubt those plundered ships were an easy thing for a former pirate to arrange."

"I knew it!" Rachel cried. "I knew somehow Mr. Craven was behind it all."

Miranda looked at Rachel without seeming to see her. "'Tis disgraceful, isn't it, that Rachel had Father figured out, and I, who should have known him better than anyone, couldn't see him for what he was."

All of a sudden Rachel understood how terrible it

must have been for Miranda to face the truth about her
father. Rachel's heart went out to her.

"What I don't understand," Papa was saying to Miranda,
"is why it was so difficult for you to tell me that Craven
was your father. Surely you didn't think that your father's
past would matter to me."

Miranda looked down. "I was afraid it would, John.
How could a man of your station wed the daughter of
a pirate?"

"Don't you see?" Rachel burst out. "Papa doesn't
care a fig about people's stations. At least he didn't
before—"

"Before I came?" Miranda gave a small, sad smile.
"I think you're right, Rachel. I think it was I who cared
about it, too much, I see now. And I was wrong to judge
your friends as I did. It sounds as if they're quite devoted
to you and very brave besides. I'm looking forward to
meeting them. Perhaps they and their mother would
come to the wedding. If there is still to be one . . ."

Would Papa still marry Miranda? To Rachel's surprise,
she realized it wouldn't bother her if Papa did. She
understood Miranda now, and it seemed that Miranda
understood Rachel. That was a start anyway. Perhaps
someday, just as Papa had said, Rachel might come to
care for Miranda as much as he did. Rachel waited for
Papa's answer.

Papa took Miranda's hand. "Certainly there'll be a

wedding," he said. "The sheriff already told me that Craven's ill-gotten gains will be distributed among those he's cheated. My share should be more than enough to save our home and reestablish my business."

Aunt Catherine sat up very straight in her chair. "I suppose we have Rachel to thank for that. If she and her friends hadn't gone to the island, Craven would have escaped, and you, John, would never have gotten your fortune back."

Emotion flickered in Papa's eyes, but it was Miranda who answered, somewhat hoarsely. "Yes, we have Rachel to thank."

"Then I'm to stay with you, too, Papa?" It was a thought that had just crossed Rachel's mind. She thought she knew the answer, but she wanted to be sure.

Papa released his hold on Miranda and took Rachel's hands in his own large, strong ones. Rachel felt his warmth spread up her arms and over her whole body. "My dear daughter," he said. "We're a family. You shall stay with me always." Papa's eyes were full of tenderness.

Against the shuttered windows the storm hammered, but the room glowed with the warm light of candle and fireside. The candles, as they melted, gave off the sweet odor of the myrtle berries from which they were made, and Rachel's mind went back, back to the island and the myrtle grove . . . to the fog and the terror of those last hours there. Then it shot forward again, here, to her home, to this room where the people who cared for her were gathered.

Rachel pulled one of her hands from Papa's and clasped it into Miranda's, so that Rachel, Miranda, and Papa were all holding hands. She saw Aunt Catherine smiling and nodding her head.

"Yes," Rachel said firmly. "We *are* a family, all of us."

1724

GOING BACK
IN TIME

Looking Back: 1724

Charles Town in Rachel's day was the busiest port in South Carolina, indeed in all the southern colonies. But Charles Town (now Charleston) also had another, more notorious, distinction: it was a favorite stopping place for pirates. The colony of South Carolina lay between two chief pirate haunts—the islands of the Caribbean and the inlets of North Carolina. The residents of Charles Town knew that pirates were law-less bandits who attacked merchant ships and stole their cargo. But in the 1600s, pirates mostly attacked wealthy Spanish ships, and since the Spaniards had often raided Charles Town, townspeople weren't terribly concerned about the pirates' dark deeds.

In fact, in Charles Town's early years (from 1680 to about 1715), the town actually welcomed pirates. Pirates brought their money to town and spent it freely in the shops and taverns. For years, pirate silver and gold was the only money in use. Merchants were happy to buy the pirates' stolen goods at cheap prices, then resell the goods to townspeople for far more money. Many merchants, like Mr. Craven, made huge fortunes this way.

By the time of Rachel's story, however, attitudes toward pirates had begun to change. At some point—historians are not sure exactly when—pirates in the Atlantic began to attack any ship they happened upon, not just Spanish ships. Charles Town merchants, of course, were outraged when their own rich cargoes ended up in pirate hands. Then, about 1721, laws were enacted that made anyone who traded with pirates a partner to their crimes. That meant that a man like Mr. Craven—or even an unsuspecting business partner like Rachel's father—could be tried and hanged for piracy. Pirates quickly began to lose their welcome in Charles Town.

Another reason that Charles Town changed its mind about pirates was a raid on the town by a pair of famous pirates—Blackbeard and "The Gentleman Pirate," Stede Bonnet. In 1718, the two pirates, with a floating army of ships, blockaded Charles Town's harbor and took prominent citizens hostage. The pirates eventually sent the hostages ashore stripped naked and sailed away. Charles Town retaliated by sending its greatest fighting man, Colonel William Rhett, after the pirates. Blackbeard escaped, but Rhett returned with Stede Bonnet as his prisoner.

Bonnet, like the fictional Mr. Craven, had once been a wealthy planter in Barbados in the West Indies, but he abandoned his wife and children for piracy. On the high seas, "The Gentleman Pirate" became feared even above Blackbeard for his cruelty.

When Colonel Rhett brought Bonnet back to Charles Town, the sheriff placed Bonnet under arrest but treated him with special courtesy because Bonnet was a man of wealth and education. Instead of putting the pirate in jail, the sheriff kept him under arrest in his own home. But Bonnet, dressed in women's clothing, escaped and made for the sea in an open boat. A sudden storm forced him back to an island, much like Skull Island, where he hid. The citizens of Charles Town hunted Bonnet down and took him back to the mainland for trial. The jury found him guilty of piracy, and "The Gentleman Pirate" went to the gallows.

Over the next decade, with tougher laws against pirates, piracy steadily declined. By 1730, most pirates had vanished from the Carolina coast. While piracy declined, Charles Town's wealth and influence grew. Colonial Charles Town was rich, so rich that visitors from the North would gasp at its lavish homes and the elegance of the fine ladies and gentlemen on the streets. Charles Town had all the liveliness of London society, coupled with the charm and beauty of the Caribbean islands. It is no wonder that Rachel quickly fell in love with her new home.

ABOUT THE AUTHOR

Elizabeth McDavid Jones grew up in North Carolina, not far from the small coastal town where the famous pirate Blackbeard once lived. She now resides in Virginia. The beautiful beaches and barrier islands of the Carolinas are a favorite vacation spot for the McDavid-Jones family, where they enjoy swimming, sunning, surfing, shelling, and kayaking.

"Liz" is also the author of six other historical mysteries for children: *The Night Flyers, Secrets on 26th Street, Watcher in the Piney Woods, Ghost Light on Graveyard Shoal, Peril at King's Creek,* and *Traitor in Williamsburg. The Night Flyers* won the 2000 Edgar Award for Best Children's Mystery, and *Ghost Light on Graveyard Shoal* was an Agatha Award finalist.

For more great fiction and nonfiction, go to windmillbooks.com.